SERVING STERLING

Sold to Sterling Book Two

EVERLY STONE

SERVING STERLING

Sold to Sterling Book Two

By Everly Stone

All Rights Reserved

Copyright **Serving Sterling** © 2021 Everly Stone

All rights reserved. Without limiting the rights under copyright reserved above, no part of this publication may be reproduced, stored in or introduced into a retrieval system, or transmitted, in any form, or by any means (electronic, mechanical, photocopying, recording, or otherwise) without the prior written permission of the copyright owner. This erotic romance is a work of fiction. Names, characters, places, brands, media, and incidents are either the product of the author's imagination or are used fictitiously. The author acknowledges the trademarked status and trademark owners of various products referenced in this work of fiction, which have been used without permission. The publication/use of these trademarks is not authorized, associated with, or sponsored by the trademark owners. This ebook is licensed for your personal use only. This ebook may not be re-sold or given away to other people. If you would like to share this book with another person, please purchase an additional copy for each person you share it with, especially if you enjoy hot, sexy, emotional novels featuring Dominant alpha males. If you are reading this book and did not purchase it, or it was not purchased for your use only, then you should return it and purchase your own copy. Thank you for respecting the author's work. Cover design by Bootstrap Designs.

✳ Created with Vellum

ABOUT THE BOOK

My new master is intense, intimidating, and wildly unpredictable.

The only thing I can count on? That he makes me ache in ways I didn't know were possible before he caught me in his web.

Sterling's secrets are of the dark and dangerous variety—there's no doubt in my mind about that now. But I still can't figure out what he truly wants from me.

He says he'll take what I've promised when "the time is right."

In the meantime, he seems determined to treat me like a naughty submissive, a princess, or...his lover.

But I can't let myself be drawn in by his generous, wickedly sexy side.

Serving Sterling is something I can survive.

Falling for Sterling would destroy me—body, heart, and soul.

Warning: Serving Sterling is the second installment in a three-book serial romance. It's a dark, dirty, boundary pushing romance that ends in a cliffhanger.

For the snow that kept me company as I wrote. You were so lovely and peaceful.

CHAPTER ONE

Sterling

Three years earlier...

I stand next to the open grave, reeling from an ugly case of déjà vu and fighting the urge to rip down the tent shielding us from the rain with my bare hands.

It's only been ten months since we were here the last time, to bury my mother.

And now Victoria lies beside her in the family plot in Queens, cut down by the same weapon.

The same poisonous son of a bitch.

Connor Potter.

"I'm going to kill him," I murmur beneath my breath to Forrest, my dry eyes fixed on the top of Vicky's coffin as mourners file by on the other side of the grave, tossing fistfuls of dirt into the open wound gouged in the earth.

"It wouldn't do any good," my brother says, his voice thin and rough.

Neither of us slept last night. We were up until dawn going through Victoria's office and laptop, searching for something we could use to destroy Connor Potter, and coming up empty. However Vicky got her hands on the drugs—from Potter himself or one of the doctors stupid or crooked enough to work with him—she didn't leave a trail behind for us to follow.

"Potter Pharm stands to make way too much money on this one," Forrest continues. "The board of directors would keep the trial going, even if Connor was dead."

I curl my hands into fists, knowing he's right but hating his defeated tone all the same. "We have to do something. He's going to kill more people before he's done, Forrest. The trial obviously isn't fucking safe."

"I talked to my connections with the FDA. They said there's nothing they can do."

"You're a top lobbyist," I snap. "Try harder."

"There haven't been any other deaths, Barrick," he says. "And Mom and Vicky both signed paperwork acknowledging that they understood the drug was experimental and could have negative side effects. Including death."

"But how many of the other patients owned property next to the Potter family beach house on Cape Ann that they refused to sell?" I ask, keeping my voice low.

The world of the obscenely wealthy is a small one. Half the people at this funeral know the Potter family personally and an even higher number know that the Potters and the Staffords have been feuding since the moment our respective families stepped off the boat.

Not the Mayflower, but both clans arrived not long after, taking their British wealth and growing it into a fortune by exploiting the resources of the new world. We're American royalty. And just like the kings and queens of old, we've done battle for riches, territory, and prestige.

The Staffords have owned several of the larger banks on the eastern seaboard for centuries. My great-great-whatever-grandfather used that money to buy up every piece of land surrounding the Potter family mansion on Cape Ann, blocking development or construction on the surrounding acreage. The Potters have been forced to use the same, single-lane dirt road to access their estate since the late 1800s.

The reason my ancestor hated the Potters enough to take such drastic steps to lower their property value has been lost to history, but I'm positive he had a good reason. As far as I can tell, the Potters have always been criminals and charlatans, making their first million selling snake oil medicines before moving into modern drug manufacturing and shady art deals in third world countries.

"The people at Potter Pharma couldn't have known about the family connection," Forrest says. "The medication was prescribed by Mom and Vicky's doctor and no patient names were given to the drug company. Just age, race, and sex of the participants."

"You really believe that? You honestly think this is all just a coincidence?"

"I don't know, Barrick. I...don't know." He drags a hand through his graying hair. At thirty-one, his hair is already nearing the salt-and-pepper stage, reminding me of our first trip to the graveyard.

Dad was only fifty when he died of a heart attack. Forrest was fourteen, I was eleven, and Vicky had just celebrated her fifth birthday. She'd cracked little jokes through the entire funeral, seemingly amused by all the somber grown-ups wearing black. I remember wishing Mom had left her at home with the nanny, and that I was there with them.

My father had been a frightening man in life—so fixated on excellence, control, and discipline that pleasing him felt next to impossible—but he was even scarier in death. Even at eleven I'd sensed that my mother wasn't up to the challenge of running our household without him. Mom was always so tired, so weak and...scattered. There were entire weeks when she didn't leave her bedroom, when the faint sound of the television droning behind her locked door was the only sign that she was still alive and the nannies refused to let us bother her, even to pop in for a hug before bed.

I'd been told that she had multiple sclerosis, but at eleven I didn't understand what that meant. It wasn't until nearly two decades later, when she was one of the first patients accepted into the Potter Pharma drug trial that I began to realize how much the disease had stolen from her.

And from us.

For a few golden months, my mother was vibrant, confident, and full of energy. Then the seizures started, followed quickly by manic episodes and withdrawal symptoms as she was weaned off the medication. She went half mad trying to get her hands on more of those pale yellow pills, desperate to feel healthy again. Eventually she found someone willing to supply her with what she craved.

The toxicology report after her death revealed she had five times the recommended dose of Vitacore in her system.

Potter Pharma refused to take any responsibility, calling my mother's negative reaction to the meds an "anomaly" and insisting they had no clue who had given her the pills. It must have been one of the doctors working with them on the trial. An internal investigation was conducted but no culprit was found.

Besides, they said, if we were so certain Vitacore was dangerous, why was our sister still a part of the trial?

Forrest and I hadn't known Victoria was on the medication, too, until the meeting with Potter Pharma's lawyers. Her MS didn't seem to be as severe as our mother's, but apparently Victoria was simply better at hiding her symptoms. Citing nightmarish days when her right side would become so weak she wasn't able to tie her shoes, let alone hold a paintbrush or properly complete her work as an art restoration specialist, Vicky insisted on remaining part of the trial.

It took longer for the poison to take our sister, but eventually the outcome was the same. Vicky didn't suffer from the negative side effects that our mother did, but she also overdosed on Vitacore. A maid found her floating face down in the bathtub of the honeymoon suite at a swanky midtown hotel.

The Potter Pharma lawyers are already insinuating that it was suicide, that our mother and sister were unstable and had undisclosed mental illnesses that made them a bad fit for the trial.

Basically, according to them, it's Mom and Vicky's fault that they're dead.

Or ours. For failing to protect our own.

On that gray morning standing beside my sister's grave, there's still enough doubt in my mind—and guilt, so much fucking guilt for being so swept up in my divorce and the demands of my work that I missed the warning signs—that I drop the subject. I follow Forrest back to his penthouse on the Upper East Side, the one he inherited when our father died, and drink cognac with distant relatives, discreetly grieving in the tradition of WASP families.

But I don't give up. I don't stop poking my nose into the details of my sister's death. And eventually, with the help of my private investigators, I come into possession of surveillance video showing Connor Potter exiting The Luxe just hours before my sister's estimated time of death. The footage came from a liquor store across the street from the hotel and was grainy and rough, but it was clearly Connor.

The footage was enough to earn Connor a visit from the NYPD, but he had an alibi—he was there meeting a drug rep for a happy hour drink—and his presence was written off as a coincidence. As was the fact that the hotel's own surveillance cameras just happened to go offline the evening that Connor and Vicky were both at The Luxe.

I suspect Connor bribed someone high up in the NYPD to make the investigation go away, but I can't prove it.

I can't prove that he killed Vicky or my mother, either, but that doesn't matter. Some things you just...know. Deep down in your bones. And I *know* that Connor Potter killed the women I loved most in the world—the latest atrocity committed in our families' feud —even though the man isn't even a "real" Potter.

Connor was adopted by Edgar Potter when Edgar married his mother, a fact that earned him brutal teasing from the other boys at our exclusive prep school. One of the upperclassmen found out that Connor's mom had never been married before and the nickname "Bastard Boy"—later shortened to B.B.—was born.

By the time Connor and I were both sophomores, I couldn't remember calling him anything but B.B.

Or asshole.

Connor and I never got along. He was too whiny, too sneaky, and too prone to public meltdowns for someone like me, who'd been raised to believe showing emotion was tantamount to shitting your pants in public. My father died when I was young, but his lessons in maintaining a stiff upper lip lingered. I had nothing but contempt for Connor Potter, and as soon as I graduated Candor Prep and headed off to college, I quickly forgot all about him.

But perhaps he never forgot me, or how small I'd made him feel when I bested him at every sport in school and trounced his pathetic attempt to take my valedictorian title without breaking a mental sweat. Could the atrocities he perpetrated against my family have roots there?

I share my suspicions with Forrest, but he tells me that I'm crazy, that people don't plot elaborate murders to get revenge for old schoolyard grudges. He's so convincing that I almost believe him.

And then I run into Connor at a garden party the following summer. He's there with his youngest stepsister, a pale redhead he clearly dotes upon. He rarely leaves her side the entire afternoon, except to queue up behind me in line for a lobster roll.

I bristle at his presence but resolve to ignore him until I overhear him say to the woman beside him, "I'm in midtown almost every Thursday. We should meet for happy hour at The Luxe sometime. They have fabulous Bloody Marys."

The casual mention of the place where my sister died wasn't a coincidence. I knew that even before I turned to face him, before his shit stain brown eyes met mine with a look that confirmed all my worst suspicions.

Connor did indeed target my mother and sister on purpose. Their blood was on his hands, and he was positive he'd gotten away with it. His confidence that he would never pay for his crimes was written in the ugly curve of his smug-as-fuck smile.

It took every ounce of control I possessed to turn back around, pretending to be unaffected. But I did it. I even forced myself to eat the lobster roll, though every bite tasted like ash in my mouth.

But as I ate and drank champagne and talked shop with the other financial world people at the party, I was silently plotting my revenge.

And watching Connor attend to his stepsister's needs with a devotion I'd never previously observed in the man...

The girl was clearly important to him, someone he loved. Maybe the *only* person he loved. He and his mother were never close, and he had miserable luck with the girls from Candor Prep's sister campus. My digging into his private life after the funeral had revealed no wife or fiancée and very few friends. Business associates and connections, yes—every person mingling at our level of society has those—but meaningful connection was scarce in Connor's world.

There was just Trudy, the bubbly redhead with the frizzy curls.

From a distance, she didn't look like much. Despite her elegant designer sundress and tasteful accessories, she seemed...unpolished, ill at ease in the company of society elites though she was raised to be one of us.

But I'd heard rumors that the Potter girls were odd, dreamy, and, in the case of the older girl, prone to embarrassing stints in rehab. That's allegedly why Edgar left control of the business to Connor in his will.

But I wasn't worried about how odd Trudy might or might not be. She was still a woman, and I'd never met one who could say "no" to me. When I wanted a woman, I had her, at least for a little while.

I began planning how to ruin the youngest Potter sister that night.

It took longer than expected to arrange for her to be at my mercy, but now she's here. On my land, in my home, and under my control.

I've paid for the privilege of breaking Connor's sweet little sister, and I intend to start tonight, no matter how my conscience pricks at me, insisting it isn't right to punish an innocent woman for her brother's sins.

But the voice of pain is louder. The howling void left behind by the loss of the two most important people in my life, of my *family*, insists on vengeance. Mercy isn't an option, Connor ensured that when he all but confessed that he'd facilitated Vicky's overdose.

ONCE WE'RE ALONE in Trudy's new room, the place where her erotic education—and eventual destruction—will take place, I don't hesitate to order her to her knees. "Take my cock out of my pants, Miss Potter," I say, holding her gaze as she blinks up at me from the floor, wearing nothing but panties and her brown boots. "Slowly."

I watch her obey, my dick swelling until I'm leaking pre-come even as my heart shrivels in my chest. I'm going to hate myself for this someday—and probably hate myself even more for enjoying it—but I've gone too far to turn back now.

The trap has been set and sprung.

It's already too late to save sweet Trudy Potter, a fact I prove as I fist my hand in her hair and say, "Hurry up, princess. I need to fuck your mouth, and I don't like to wait. If you want to avoid that spanking we talked about in the car, I need to see your lips wrapped around my cock. Now."

I'm a bad man, there's no doubt about that, but the heat mixing with the anxiety in her pale green eyes helps quiet the regret whispering through my chest.

She wants this. Her hot little pussy is probably already dripping down her thighs.

I'm not destroying this girl; I'm merely giving her access to something dangerous that she craves. She's going to destroy *herself*, just like my mother and Vicky allegedly did.

This is poetic justice.

It's also wrong and repulsive and...hot as fucking hell.

"That's right," I murmur as she reaches for the top of my boxer briefs, letting lust take over, banishing my shame. "Now put your mouth on me, princess. I'll show you what to do and then, if you're a good girl, I'll take care of you after."

And I will.

I will take care of Trudy...right up until the day I destroy her.

CHAPTER TWO

Trudy

Fear and desire merge and explode in my chest as I draw his boxers down with trembling hands, revealing the thick head of his cock.

God. He's huge. Even bigger than I guessed when I was rubbing against him in the museum and in the private room at Persephone's.

Pulse thready in my throat, I work his pants and boxers down, lower and lower, until I expose his entire massive, swollen erection.

Once it's free, the length and girth of him is flat-out *terrifying*.

But also...beautiful. Potent. And so sexy my nipples bead into tingling points as I guide his pants down his thighs. The sight of him so hard—veins standing out along the ridge of his shaft and pre-come glistening at his tip—and knowing *I'm* the reason for his arousal is indescribably hot.

Hot enough to make me squirm and my thighs clench together as I watch him step out of his pants, his cock bobbing gently as he moves.

"Lick it." He steps closer, cradling my head in his hands as he brushes a thumb over my bottom lip. "Lick the come off my tip, princess. See if you like the taste."

Sucking in a bracing breath, I rest my hands on his powerful thighs and lean in, dragging my tongue slowly over the top of him, a soft sound of surprise escaping my lips as I caress his burning flesh.

"Well?" he asks, watching me with hooded eyes that make the hunger building low in my belly intensify and my erect nipples even more desperate for his touch.

"Your skin is so hot," I whisper. "Like you're running a fever."

"I am," he murmurs. "And there's only one cure. Fuck, Trudy, open your mouth, I can't wait another second to be inside you."

Eyes wide, I ignore the voice of doom insisting I'm going to be as terrible at this the second time as I was the first and drop my jaw.

Sterling grunts in response, an almost amused sound that makes my eyes roll up to lock with his.

"Not wide enough?" I part my lips a little farther, until my jaw starts to ache.

He shakes his head. "You really are clueless when it comes to sex, aren't you, princess?"

"Mostly, yes," I confess, my gaze shifting to the swollen length of him and then back to his face. "But I know not to use my teeth. I'm supposed to cover them with my lips and suck, not blow. Right?"

He mutters something that might have been "unbelievable," but before I can apologize again, he grips my arms and pulls me to my feet. "On the bed, Potter. It seems we need to start with the basics."

"No, I can do it. I promise, I—" My words end in a gasp as he cups my breasts roughly in his hands, pinching my nipples tight enough to send electricity surging straight between my legs.

"Don't argue with me, Trudy," he rumbles. "Just get up on the bed."

"Yes, sir," I say, moaning as he rolls my nipples between his fingers again and again, building the hunger already throbbing, thick and heavy, between my hip bones.

"Good girl." His hand drops between my

legs, sliding through my slickness and then back to circle my clit with a casual ownership that makes me tremble.

By the time he pulls his hand away and gives me a sharp swat on my bottom—clearly an invitation to get moving—I'm starved for him again, ready to do whatever it takes to prove that I can give him the same kind of satisfaction he gives me.

I might be an inexperienced virgin, but I'm a fast learner, especially when a subject has captured my interest.

And Sterling, climbing into bed beside me, naked and stunning and clearly in desperate need of relief, has *thoroughly* captured my interest.

CHAPTER THREE

Sterling

After a quick lesson in how to suck cock, my clueless virgin seems to be getting the hang of things.

Damn, is she getting the hang of things...

"Like this again?" Trudy's tongue slips from between her lips. She licks my cock from base to tip before pausing to circle my swollen, suffering head, lapping away the fluid leaking from my tip.

"Yes," I murmur. "Just like that."

My balls are so full, so heavy that I can barely breathe and I'm so desperate to come my heart is throbbing in my throat.

But I don't want this lesson to be over so soon.

I don't know what's hotter—watching Trudy gain the confidence to explore a man's body or feeling her tongue on my cock—but I've rarely experienced anything more erotic. And then her lips part. She sucks me into the heat of her mouth for the first time and my vision blurs.

I curse beneath my breath as my head falls back on the pillows. My hips lift of their own accord, too desperate for more of her sweetness to resist plunging deeper.

Trudy moans in response and suckles me harder, repositioning herself so that she's between my spread legs and her nipples brush against my thighs as she leans forward. Getting her on the bed was the best call—she relaxed as soon as I was laid out beneath her instead of looming over her with my hand in her hair—but it might also be my downfall.

How the hell am I going to resist her?

How am I going to limit this to a blow job designed to show her who's in control, when I'm dying to roll her beneath me, spread her legs, and drive my cock inside her hot little cunt?

I want to take her, to claim her, to mark her with hot streams of come shot into her untried body. I want to watch her expression bloom with shock and betrayal as she realizes I won't be using a condom, and that she'd better hope whatever precautions she's taken previously are enough to keep me from putting a bastard in her belly.

The thought of fucking her bare makes me even harder—it's always been a kink for me, one I've rarely had the chance to indulge—but we're not even close to that stage of our evolution.

There are so many smaller wounds to inflict before I deliver that final blow.

Which means I need to stop thinking with my dick and start thinking like a man focused on revenge. My vengeful side is disgusted with this display of patient sensual education, insisting it's time to knock Trudy off-balance and ensure she goes to sleep tonight wondering if she's just made the biggest mistake of her life.

Forcing a note of impatience into my voice, I mutter, "Enough. I'll do it myself, roll over. On your back."

She lifts her head, my cock popping from between her lips with a sexy sound that makes more pre-come leak from my tip. "But I—"

"On your back," I growl. "Now. This is the last time I'll remind you to follow orders. The next time you question me, you'll be punished, Miss Potter."

Eyes wide, she rolls onto her back, her arms crossed over her chest to conceal her breasts and her thighs locked together, which won't do at all.

I need to see her.

My eyes are starved for another glimpse of her slick, swollen pussy.

Coming onto my knees, I reach down, guiding her thighs apart before I kneel between them, taking my dick in hand. "Play with your tits again, Trudy," I say, starting to jerk my shaft as I keep my eyes fixed on her chest, deliberately refusing to look in her wounded eyes.

She obeys—stiffly and with very little enthusiasm—but she brings her fingers to her nipples, rolling them in circles as I pump my shaft harder, faster, knowing I need to come before I lose my erection.

I'm not a sadist in real life; I'm just playing one until Connor Potter learns what it feels like to have someone he loves destroyed. I don't get off on shaming the woman in my bed but having Trudy off-balance and doubting her sexual prowess is necessary to my endgame.

The more ways I can break her down, the better. Every nick in her confidence is a step toward forming a handhold I can use to rip her apart.

"We'll try again tomorrow, Miss Potter," I say flatly, keeping my face as expressionless as possible as I near the edge. "See if you can't learn what to do with that pretty mouth." My hand is flying now and my breath coming fast as I add, "Open your mouth. Stick your tongue out. Now. Right fucking now."

She obeys a second before I come like a freight train careening off the rails, all the built-up pressure in my balls from the erotically torturous afternoon ensuring the first burst of my release reaches my intended target. My come splashes into her face, making her blink and sputter as it slides into her eyes and mouth. She reaches up to wipe at her eyes, leaving her breasts bare and ready to receive the rest of my release. I watch my seed splatter across her milky white skin and remind myself that it's okay to be turned on by it.

There's no place for shame in this bargain.

The course has been set and Trudy bought and paid for.

She entered into this agreement of her own free will and she's free to go any time she wants.

But she won't. I know she won't.

Because I'm going to keep her too fucked in the head, too torn between misery and bliss, to think clearly.

"Next time you'll take it down your

throat." I place the heel of my hand over her clit, rubbing her hard as I smear my fingers through my own come to capture her nipple. "I'll fuck your mouth and you'll take every drop, Trudy. Won't you?" I pinch her nipple, summoning a confused, but turned-on sound from her parted lips. "You'll swallow me like a good girl and ask for more because that's the only way you get this, princess. Next time, you're going to have to work harder if you want to get off."

"Oh, God," she whimpers, bucking into my hand. "God!"

"That's not my name, sweetheart," I say as she gasps and writhes even more shamelessly beneath me. "When you come, you say *my* name, no one else's. Because your orgasms belong to me, princess, every fucking one."

"Yes, Sterling, yes!" she cries, her fingers fisting in the quilt beneath her as she spirals out, coming hard on my hand.

I fight a smile.

Already so obedient and we're just getting started.

This is going to be even easier than I assumed, so easy I would feel guilty, but there's no room for that in my sick new reality, either.

With that in mind, I slide off the bed

while Trudy's chest is still heaving and her breath coming fast. By the time she realizes I'm gone, I have my boxers and pants on and am nearly to the door.

"Wait, I..." She trails off.

I turn to face her, watching her throat work for a beat before I arch a cool brow. "Yes?"

"I...I thought you were going to give me a bath," she says, her already pink cheeks flushing a deeper rose.

"Baths are for good girls who get A's on their assignments. That was a B-minus blow job, Trudy. At best."

"I tried. I promise," she says before adding in a steadier voice, "And I'm not a girl; I'm a woman."

"Not yet, princess," I say, relishing the heat that flickers in her eyes. I can't tell if she's angry, turned on, or both, but I'm glad to see she still has some fire left in her. "But one day. Maybe. If you study hard and show me what a good student you can be. Breakfast is at seven. Don't be late. You'll need a full belly for what I have planned for you tomorrow. Sleep well."

I turn and leave, ignoring the outraged huff from the goddess on the bed.

Sitting in the middle of the navy and white quilt, wearing nothing but the afterglow of the orgasm I just gave her, with her red curls wild and her eyes shining, she is easily one of the most beautiful things I've ever seen.

Beautiful and sexy as hell.

It's a shame I'll never be able to let her know just how much I appreciate her charms, but not as much of a shame as it would be to leave my mother's and sister's murders unavenged.

Holding that thought close, I quicken my pace down the hallway, determined to find something to take my mind off Trudy Potter for the rest of the night.

In my room, I quickly change into a pair of workout shorts and a t-shirt and head for my home gym at the back of the pool house. I run and lift and crunch until I'm soaked with sweat and my body is too weary to do anything but sleep.

But I still wake in the middle of the night from a dream featuring Trudy straddling my face, bucking into my mouth as I feast on her sweetness.

She's already haunting my subconscious.

It's a bad sign.

I know that, even before I head down-stairs early the next morning, still sore from my punishing workout, to find the dining room empty. A beat later I hear voices murmuring downstairs. I descend the staircase into the kitchen to find Trudy up to her elbows in some sort of dough and laughing with Harlow in the warm, sugar-scented kitchen.

Laughing. With *Harlow.*

Harlow has worked for me for nearly five years, and I've never once seen her laugh. She rarely even smiles. She's as serious as they come, a fifty-something Romanian immigrant who escaped a bad marriage—and poverty in her home country—on her cooking skills alone. Therefore, she takes the business of planning and preparing meals seriously. Very seriously.

But here she is, giggling like a schoolgirl as Trudy tells her a story about getting lost at an Oktoberfest celebration in Munich and ending up wearing a pretzel costume on a float.

"And every time this one section of the music played, mustard would shoot out of hidden spouts in the plastic flowers behind me," Trudy says. "By the time I finally found my friends at the end of the parade route, I was yellow from head to toe. It took days to get the smell out of my hair."

"Sounds like Oktoberfest," Harlow says, her usually steady, practical monotone still dancing with laughter. "When I was small, my father still had family in Germany. We'd visit them every few years. Always in October. The grown-ups would drink too much beer and the kids would run wild and stay up until midnight. We loved it."

"Sounds like fun," I murmur, ambling across the kitchen to stand on the other side of the large marble island.

Harlow's spine straightens in response, her smile fading as she pulls on a pair of oven mitts. "Good morning, Mr. Sterling. The quiche is coming out of the oven now, and the Dutch baby with peaches is about to go in. I wasn't expecting you for another forty minutes, sir."

"I have some business to take care of in my office. Take your time." I shift my focus to Trudy, whose smile has also vanished. She looks anxious and embarrassed, a state of being that intensifies as I nod over my shoulder and say, "Follow me, please, Trudy. I have a few questions for you."

"Yes, sir," she mumbles as she brushes the dough and flour off her hands and turns to wash them in the large sink behind her.

Once her back is to us, Harlow shoots me a look I can't quite decipher, but is firmly in the "disapproving" category. I've never brought a woman home to Rooky Wood before, let alone one so young, beautiful, or obviously uncomfortable in my presence. Perhaps Harlow thinks I should find a woman closer to my own age. Or one who actually enjoys my company.

Whatever her thoughts, I doubt I'll ever learn them. I don't make a habit of consulting my staff for their opinions on my sex life *or* my revenge plans.

Making a mental note to remind Harlow of the nondisclosure agreement she signed when she came to work for me—can't have her carrying tales of my anxious young lover to the village gossips that might reach my brother, who would figure out my nefarious intentions in about five seconds—I start toward my office by the sitting room, trusting Trudy will follow.

I settle behind my desk, reminding myself that her unhappiness this morning is all part of my plan. Still, when she appears a few moments later, her fingers gripping the trim around the door as she leans against one side of the frame—clearly less than thrilled to be joining me—my jaw tightens.

I don't like inspiring fear and loathing in the opposite sex. I don't have much experience with it, either. Women tend to like me— quite a bit. Aside from a few ugly meetings with our lawyers, during which Celia held forth on my flaws in excruciating detail, even my ex-wife finds me fairly agreeable.

She ought to, considering how many millions I parted with to be free of her.

But I don't care about the money. There's always more of it to be made. Parting with large sums of cash isn't something that concerns me.

I may, in fact, end up giving *this* woman millions, as well, if she ends up pregnant after our first and only night together and chooses to have the baby. I will happily pay child support for eighteen years. It will give me joy, in fact, to know Connor's watching my bastard grow up as fatherless and uncared for by his or her sire as he was as a child.

And it's not as if the kid will be missing out on much. He or she will have my money. In my experience, that's the best of what the Stafford men have to offer. Forrest and I are both detached and withdrawn, just like our father, and what child wants a dad like that?

I certainly didn't when I was small. But now I'm grateful for the hard lessons my father taught me. He helped make me strong enough to survive in a merciless world.

He made me one of the predators instead of the prey.

Watching my prey cling to the doorframe for dear life, I silently thank him for it. I might not laugh nearly as much as this woman, but I won't shed a tear after she's gone, either.

But *she* will. I'll make sure of it.

I force a smile and motion her over. "Come. I need your assistance with a few things. I won't bite."

Her lips pucker and shift to one side.

My smile widens. "I won't. I promise. No biting until at least nine a.m. And I prefer to have my coffee first."

She exhales a soft laugh and steps gingerly into the room. "Good to know. I asked Harlow if it was okay to come down to the kitchen, by the way, like you said, to make sure I wouldn't be bothering her."

"Perfect. I'm sure she appreciated that. She seems to like you."

"Well, I'm very likeable," Trudy says, her features relaxing a bit more when I laugh and agree, "You are."

That's another thing my father taught me —how confusing and ultimately heartbreaking it can be for someone to shower you with time, trust, and attention one day only to turn around and find you irritating and unpleasant for months on end.

Trudy and I don't have months, but I trust the technique will work on a slightly tighter timeline. And who knows, maybe she *will* be with me for months. If I can keep my dick out of her hot little pussy for that long...

My cock thickens at the thought, and I elect to stay seated as Trudy comes to hover beside my chair.

I point to my laptop screen. "I'm having a few things sent over from town. I'll need your sizes and color preferences."

She leans closer, but not too close. She's clearly in no hurry to touch me again. Her natural protective instincts are kicking in, but that's fine. It will only make it that much more satisfying when I override them.

"Riding clothes?" she asks, straightening swiftly and taking a step back as I swivel my chair to face her. "Thank you, but I don't need riding clothes. I can ride in jeans and a sweatshirt. It's what I wore most of the time as a kid. We only put on the fancy stuff when my grandmother came to spend the weekend. She was fussy about things like that."

"Really? You kept horses growing up?" I arch a brow and feign ignorance about her upbringing.

Persephone's Closet does a background check on all their escorts, but that's only to ensure the women don't have a criminal record or pose a threat to their customers. The girls are allowed to keep their private lives private if they choose.

Or at least as private as the internet will allow.

I do have Trudy's full name, after all, and could have done my own poking around in her past. But I prefer for her to believe I didn't bother. That I was so unconcerned with who she is that I didn't take the time to peruse her social media let alone dig any deeper into her personal history.

"Yes," she replies, sadness creeping into her expression as she adds, "But we sold them after my mother died. My father found animals...overwhelming. And then we moved to the city so..."

"You were young when she died?" I ask, wondering how much she'll confide in me. If our positions were reversed, I wouldn't give her a scrap of personal information, not a single solitary fact that might make me more vulnerable than I was already.

But Trudy is far more trusting than I've ever been, a fact she proves when she nods. "I was eight."

"I'm sorry. I was eleven when my father died." I've planned to share this with her—it's a shared experience I expect will create a sense of closeness between us that I can use to my advantage—but I'm surprised by how natural it feels to speak the words. I never talk about that time of my life, not even with my brother or my sister before she passed.

Her brow furrowing, Trudy reaches out, resting a gentle hand on my shoulder. "I'm sorry. It's so hard to lose a parent when you're little. It makes the world feel...unsafe in a way I'm not sure you can ever really shake."

"But maybe that's for the best," I counter. "The world *isn't* safe. That's reality."

"But kids don't know that. And they aren't ready to know that. It's too much, too soon. Like putting a saddle on a foal. You wouldn't do that. You'd hurt them, maybe even ruin them for life."

"So, you're saying we're...ruined?"

Her lips quirk up on one side as she pulls her hand from my shoulder and crosses her arms over her chest. "Well, clearly. I mean, at least *you* are."

Her words surprise me, but then my prey has already proven she has a feisty side. "Really? And what's your evidence for this, Miss Potter?"

"I'm still gathering evidence, Mr. Sterling, but the preliminary findings suggest a fear of intimacy and an aversion to meaningful human connection," she says, wrinkling her nose as she adds in a stage whisper, "Spoiler alert, but normal, healthy people don't buy virgins for half a million dollars."

Amused, though I probably shouldn't be, I cross my arms, mimicking her pose as I challenge, "And normal, healthy women don't usually hold on to their V cards until nearly thirty years of age."

"I'm only twenty-five," she huffs.

"That rounds up to thirty. And it's odd, especially for someone who's not only beautiful and charming but also seems to enjoy coming quite a bit." I shrug. "At least in my experience."

She blushes, but she doesn't break eye contact. "Yeah, well, maybe I'm just picky. Did you think about that? Or maybe this is all part of my master plan."

"Your master plan? And what is that?"

"If I told you, I'd have to kill you," she says, uncertainty creeping into her eyes again. "I'm just joking."

"About the master plan?" I ask.

"No. About killing you. I'm a pacifist. And I'm hoping maybe...you are too?"

I smile, a slow, lazy grin that isn't meant to be reassuring. "That's a smart thing to hope."

Her eyes narrow and she studies me for a beat before she whispers, "I'm not going to be afraid of you. Just FYI. I decided last night that I'm not going down that road. If you cross the line from grouchy, cold, and kinky to openly threatening, I'll leave. There's only so much I'm willing to put up with, Mr. Sterling, even for half a million dollars."

I arch a brow. "Grouchy, cold, and kinky?"

"At least in my experience," she says, tossing my words back at me. "But there may be more to you. I'm open to that."

I bite my bottom lip, resisting the urge to pull her into my lap and tease her sensitive nipples until she's off center again. Her confidence this morning is a good thing.

It also plays right into *my* master plan, so I'll allow it. For now.

Hell, I'll even encourage it.

"Noted, princess," I murmur. "Now, can you please give me your shirt, pant, and shoe size so I can coldly and kinkily buy you some riding clothes for our adventure this afternoon?"

Her brows lift. "Adventure?"

"I thought I'd take you on a riding tour of the property. Show you all my favorite places to lurk and grouch."

She laughs, a soft, but delightful sound, I can't help enjoying. "I like joking Sterling."

"And I like your laugh," I say, noting how quickly her smile springs to her face this time.

The poor thing. She really is going to make this too easy.

"Size small for the top," she murmurs. "Medium or size six for the bottoms and size eight for the shoes."

I nod. "Thank you. I'll have the order sent to your room when it arrives. Meet me at the stables at noon. I'll bring a picnic so we can have lunch out on the property."

"A picnic?" she asks, clasping her hands together in delight. "It's such a gorgeous day outside. That sounds amazing."

"It does," I agree, already anticipating how lovely she'll look spread out naked on a blanket under the blue autumn sky while I deliver her next lesson in how to please her master.

I'm going to have Trudy's pleasure for lunch and her fear for dinner and top it off with a little humiliation-laced orgasming right before bed.

My sweet little princess won't know what hit her.

But I will, and I intend to keep the bombs falling until she greets every morning at my home in a state of high anxiety, wondering which Sterling she's going to find when she comes downstairs—the one who means her pleasure or the one who's quickly becoming an expert in handing out pain.

CHAPTER FIVE

Trudy

Sterling takes his breakfast in his office and then disappears to places unknown. I linger in the kitchen over coffee for as long as possible—hoping to gently pump Harlow for information on her mysterious employer—but she's busy chopping vegetables and marinating various things and goes quiet every time the conversation circles back to Sterling.

She doesn't seem afraid to talk about him, per se, but she clearly has some firm boundaries in place when it comes to her employer.

The most telling thing I learn from Harlow is that Sterling is a very generous man. "He pays me more than any position I've ever had. Including the years I worked in the White House kitchen."

"You worked at the White House?" I ask, my eyes going wide over the rim of my freshly refilled mug. "That's so cool. Which presidency?"

"I can't talk about it," she says, her brow furrowing as she plops several freshly washed carrots onto her cutting board. "But I can talk about your allergies. Mr. Sterling said you had several. Could you make me a list, so I know what to avoid as I'm planning menus for the week?"

Surprised—and comforted—by the fact that Sterling cares enough about my well-being not to want me breaking out in hives in his kitchen, I explain my various sensitivities before assuring Harlow, "But if I accidentally eat an onion or red pepper, it won't kill me, just make me puffy and uncomfortable for a while."

"We don't want that," Harlow says with a small smile. "I can work with those restrictions. It won't be a problem. I just need to do a few substitutions. Onions are in many things."

"They are," I agree, watching her swiftly chop the carrots into tiny little squares. I'm hoping to catch her attention and continue the conversation, but she seems done with me for the moment.

I thank her for the lovely breakfast and excuse myself, heading up to my room to shower, even though I showered last night before I went to sleep. I needed to get the smell—and the stickiness—of Sterling off my skin before I slipped between the sheets.

The thought sends worry creeping back to tighten my shoulders.

Who is the real Sterling? The jerk who made me feel like a complete failure as a seductress—and a woman—last night? Or the charmer with the dry sense of humor I met this morning?

Maybe they're *both* real. Maybe lots of men enjoy coming on a woman's face and chest like she's a wad of tissue one minute and purchasing gifts and planning thoughtful adventures for her the next.

I wish I had more experience with men. And sex.

I have a very strong feeling I *shouldn't* have enjoyed Sterling jerking off on me the way he did. It should have felt degrading and awful. And it *did* feel that way. Sort of. But it also made me hot, made my nipples tingle and ache for his touch and my pussy even wetter.

Maybe I'm a bit of a kinky human myself...

If I stick around Sterling's mansion for

very long, I have a feeling I'm going to find out.

Filled with an equal mixture of anticipation and foreboding, I start the water in the shower and strip off the yoga pants and t-shirt I wore to bed. This shower is purely for curl-taming purposes, so I don't worry about lathering up all over. I simply drag the conditioner through my damp locks with my fingers, coil it up into a pile on my head to let it soak up the moisture, and close my eyes, letting the hot spray soothe away the last of my lingering dread.

Sterling seems to be in a good mood today. I'll enjoy that while it lasts and try not to take his grouchiness personally if Alpha Asshole makes an appearance later today. Whatever forces of nurture and nature combined to make Sterling cold, cranky, and kinky, they have very little to do with me.

He simply is who he is.

I'm not here to change him. I'm here to have sex with him or to flip him the bird and head for the exit if he proves too much for me to handle.

In the sunny light of morning, there's no doubt in my mind that he'll let me leave. We're not alone here, after all, and Harlow and Wells both seem like decent people. They wouldn't turn a deaf ear to a woman screaming for help from a cage in the basement.

Hmmm...

Cages in the basement...

I *did* see an ominous-looking door in the kitchen this morning, one that seemed to lead to a still lower level of the house, judging by the damp-earth smell seeping from around its edges. But I didn't have a chance to open it let alone explore.

As I dry off, I make a mental note to do so at the first opportunity, to explore all of Sterling's sizable mansion to see what secrets it might be willing to share. A person's home can tell you a lot about them. Their likes, their dislikes, the chances that they're going to want to strap you to some exotic sex bench and spank you with weird props...

But you wouldn't mind if he spanked you with his hand...would you?

"Yes, I would," I mutter to my reflection as I smooth curl cream through my damp hair. But my cheeks are flushed, and my eyes are glittering.

That isn't the face of a woman who's dreading her next encounter with her master's kinky side. That's the face of a woman who can't wait to see what kind of exotic fuckery is around the next corner. I had no idea this side of myself existed and it's a little...scary.

I'm in trouble.

Or I will be, if I don't keep at least one foot firmly on the ground.

With that in mind, I grab my cell from beside the sink and pull up my text thread with Millie, wondering how her check-in process went. But I don't have any bars and Millie probably wouldn't be able to reply even if I did. The rehab patients aren't allowed to communicate with friends and family until their therapists believe they're ready, and that doesn't happen on day one.

I settle for scrolling through my photos, reminding myself of all the things that matter in my life—my work, my friends, the kids I'm helping every day—and then set my phone down, wrap up in a towel, and head back into my room to find...

Christmas morning.

No, better than Christmas morning.

When I was a kid, we only received one present each. My father didn't believe in big displays for the holidays and, after my mother died, always bought Millie and me the same thing. The matching presents were often lovely but never chosen just for us. They were generic "girl child" presents that ignored how different Millie and I were as well as the fact that, as a young kid, I would have preferred the gifts Dad and my stepmother chose for Connor.

I was a tomboy, a girl who loved running wild in the woods, climbing trees, making mud pies, and plotting how I could grow up and become a pirate, but without hurting people. I didn't want to loot or pillage; I just wanted to steer my own ship and live by my own rules and have a pet parrot who said funny things.

And maybe a peg leg. At eleven, a peg leg seemed kind of cool.

I still have a bit of a thing for pirates, but by the time I was sixteen, I was also into clothes and shoes and all the "girly" things Millie had always loved.

Sixteen-year-old me would have run around this room squealing with joy, tossing box tops and tissue paper into the air.

Instead, I press a fist to my mouth, nibbling on my knuckle as I approach the stack of fancy, gift-wrapped boxes on the bench at the base of the bed with a certain degree of decorum. After all, Sterling could have picked out a bunch of fussy, stiff riding clothes in muted beiges and grays that aren't exciting at all.

But I know better.

Even before I lift the first box top to reveal a gorgeous burnt orange riding jacket with dark silver buckles and a sassy little bustle in the back that's going to look incredible flared out across the back of a saddle, I know Sterling would never choose something boring or unflattering. Sterling has impeccable taste. It's obvious from his home to his car to his own wardrobe.

"And you," I murmur as I hold the coat up in front of myself in the full-length mirror in the corner of the room, marveling at the way the color complements my hair and complexion.

"He has high standards and a taste for luxury. You wouldn't be here if he didn't think you were classy and gorgeous, girl. Don't forget that or let him make you feel small when he's in asshole mode," I whisper, meeting my own gaze in the mirror and willing myself to believe the words.

I need confidence more now than I ever have before.

Sterling is a smart, sexy, successful man who's accustomed to getting exactly what he wants, and I'm a woman who's always been eager to please. It would be so easy to fall into a powerless position with him. But my gut assures me that the best way to please Sterling is to believe in myself, to stand strong when he challenges me, and to make it clear that I value myself as much—*more*—than he did when he dropped half a million dollars for my hymen.

I roll my shoulders back and narrow my eyes. "You've got this. Don't doubt it."

Spirits buoyed by my banter with Sterling this morning and the pampering—by the time I unwrap all the boxes, I'm the proud owner of at least ten thousand dollars of gorgeous, designer riding clothes—I actually enjoy doing my makeup. Most days, I resent the twenty minutes it takes to "put on a face" donors will take seriously, but today I'm smiling as I blend eyeshadow and line the top of my lids with a dark brown smudge that looks incredible with the orange coat.

When I'm done, I stand in front of the full-length mirror again, taking in the final picture. From my new supple brown leather riding boots, to the skintight beige pants, to the slinky brown turtleneck and my fancy new coat, I look...expensive. Elegant. Like I belong in a house as impressive as this one.

I come from money, and I run in social circles jam-packed with New York City's rich and famous, but I've always secretly felt like an imposter. Like the girl who didn't belong.

When I was little, it was my fire-engine red hair, see-through pale skin, and tomboy ways that set me apart from the other girls at my expensive private school. When I was older, it was rumors of my big sister's drug and boy habits—and my tendency to wander around with my nose stuck in a book and no clue what was popular at any given moment—that made me an outcast.

In college I had a few close girlfriends and one serious boyfriend. That was the extent of my "circle of influence," and I liked it that way.

Rejoining the charity garden party and gala scene when I returned home with my degree was exhausting. But Connor insists that I attend at least one or two events a month with him as his plus-one. He says it's important that the community sees us as united in the wake of Dad's death.

People were gossiping, he said, insisting Millie and I should have at least been invited to join the board of Potter Pharma, if not appointed joint CEOs. That Connor, the stepson, slipped into the top spot and Millie and I got "modest" monetary settlements, instead, rubbed a lot of old-school society the wrong way.

Most of the rich people I know are cliquish to the point that they might as well all be living in medieval England. They will only network with, befriend, and marry other people with money and the older the money is, the better. Connor's grandparents were wealthy, but his mother squandered nearly their entire fortune on designer clothes and private jets before she married my dad.

Being new money was bad enough, but new, irresponsible money was beyond the pale.

I was too young to understand all the gossip I overheard at home, but I know Connor had a hard time when he transferred from public school to the prep school Dad offered to pay for. He was teased, ignored, and bullied, and all the old-money boys blocked him from joining their fraternities.

When I'm frustrated with how cold and cynical my stepbrother can be, I try to remember how hard it's been for him to fit in and usher compassion into my heart. But it isn't easy. Unlike Sterling, Connor doesn't have a secretly charming, humorous side.

Though now that I think about it...

Sterling might be older than he looks, but as far as I can tell, he and Connor are about the same age. And I'm willing to bet my new riding coat that Sterling comes from money and isn't simply a self-made man. His manners and way of speaking are too posh to have been acquired later in life. He reminds me of all the other powerful, successful men from wealthy New York families I've known in my life.

And those men all went to the same school.

Candor Prep and its sister campus for girls, Swallings Prep, are the best of the best. All the wealthy families in the city send their kids there, even if they have to bribe the headmaster with lavish gifts for the campus when their child's test scores aren't high enough.

Though surely if Sterling ran with that crowd, I would have seen him before that night in the museum.

But I've made a habit of avoiding parties and social gatherings as much as possible, and I'm a total workaholic. I also lost my mother long before the age when high-society ladies get together to plot which of their offspring might be a good fit to pair up. My stepmother was never accepted by the other ladies who lunch, and even if she had been, Dorey didn't have much interest in Millie or me.

She was never mean; she simply ignored

us, leaving our upbringing to our nannies and seeming vaguely surprised to see us when we showed up at mandatory Friday night family dinners or allowed our games of pretend to bleed downstairs into her domain.

She lives in the Caribbean now. I'm not sure which island. I'm not sure even Connor knows. As soon as my dad died and Dorey received her own million-dollar inheritance, she couldn't leave her old life behind fast enough.

Maybe I'll do that someday, when Millie is stable, and I've found great people to run the day-to-day aspects of the foundation in my place.

Maybe I'll go somewhere far away and reinvent myself as someone new, a brave, bold adventurer who isn't defined by her relationship to her complicated family or their money or their problems. I'll just be Trudy, a curious, compassionate, fun-loving woman who looks damned good in burnt orange.

Making a mental note to thank Sterling for introducing me to this fabulous color I've always been certain was a bad idea for redheads of my particular shade, I pad softly to my bedroom door and open it a crack.

The hall is empty, and I still have over an hour before I'm supposed to meet Sterling by the stables. Plenty of time to find a patch of cell service and do some cyber sleuthing.

Sterling knows my full name, everything that was on my Persephone's Closet intake form, as well as whatever he might decide to dig up online. My social media and internet presence are tame and non-revealing by design, but at least he has the option to explore them.

I should have the same options.

Assuring myself even Alpha Asshole Sterling can't fault me for wanting to make sure the man who bought me isn't a felon with a habit of misplacing girlfriends or beating puppies, I creep slowly down to the ground floor.

CHAPTER SIX

Trudy

I have high hopes—and the racing pulse to prove I have very little experience with snooping.

Unfortunately, after a tour of every room on the ground floor and signal-seeking on the lavish back patio, I still have no new intelligence on my buyer and no bars. But I have discovered something curious in Sterling's allegedly internet-free home—his laptop, which he used to order my clothes from a website.

No doubt about it, he was definitely online this morning.

If I hadn't been so off-balance worrying about how weird things were between us the night before, I would have noticed the discrepancy right away.

The lie, Trudy, my inner voice pipes up. *Call it what it is. He lied to you to keep you isolated and disconnected from your old life.*

And you know who does stuff like that?

Abusive, controlling men who have bad intentions, that's who.

Or men who don't want you getting online to dig into their history and find out all the morally bankrupt things they've done in their terrible, no good, really awful lives.

The inner voice could have a point, but before I jump to conclusions—or freak myself out and make a run for the main road—I should at least try to see if there's anything awful to find.

And Sterling did say I could use the landline in his office…

After a careful glance up and down the hall outside the open office door, I slip in and softly shut the door behind me. Then I hurry across the room, pulling the phone at the corner of the desk closer to the laptop so I can snatch it and pretend to be dialing if anyone comes in.

I open the laptop, but there's a lock screen, and I don't know Sterling well enough to make an educated guess as to what his password might be. I search the tidy top of the desk, but there's nothing password-revealing on the notepad beside the computer or the small stack of paperwork in a tray at the far corner.

The top drawers are also a bust, revealing nothing personal at all aside from some bright blue paperclips that hint at an appreciation for color I wouldn't have suspected, judging from the neutral-toned clothes I've seen Sterling wear so far.

I'm about to give up on snooping and place a call to Bradford, my bestie, right-hand man at Notes of Hope, and a whiz at ferreting out background information on both donors and blind dates alike, when I slide open the bottom drawer to find a stack of photo albums with a funeral program on top. A beautiful young woman with Sterling's ice-blue eyes and dark, expressive eyebrows smiles up from the front.

Glancing back to the door, I lift the heavy cardstock and flip through the program, chest tightening as a quick scan of the obituary reveals Victoria Sterling Stafford was Sterling's little sister. And that she was only twenty-two when she died.

He's lost his father and his sister.

And his mother, I realize, as I do a closer read of the surviving family members. Victoria is survived only by her brothers Forrest Sterling Stafford and Barrick Sterling Stafford. Which means Stafford wasn't Victoria's married name and my Sterling is either Forrest or Barrick.

There's a picture of the two men—Sterling, and an equally striking slightly older man with kind eyes—with Victoria, the three of them smiling on a yacht surrounded by crystal blue water.

Feeling guilty for invading his privacy but also justified—he *has* been lying to me or at the very least withholding pertinent information—I put the program back in the drawer and pick up the phone. I punch in the number to the Notes of Hope main office, thankful I have it memorized. I type in Bradford's line and wait for his mailbox message to finish.

It's Saturday, so he won't receive this message for two more days, but as soon as he does, I know he'll be on the case like white on rice. He's an amazing event organizer and mailing coordinator, but Bradford's true passion is for gossip.

"Hey, Bradford," I whisper, keeping my voice soft, just in case, "I'm out of the office unplugging at a cabin upstate this week and I don't have internet. But I met two interesting men, Barrick Sterling Stafford and his brother, Forrest. I think they might be good donor candidates. Can you do the full donor background check on them?" I take a breath, willing my tone to remain casual, "And get the personal dirt, too, just in case. Thanks so much, babes. I'll call on Tuesday or Wednesday to see what you've dug up. Have a great week!"

I hang up, my stomach churning as I imagine Bradford's squeal of excitement when he hears that message. He's been after me to get serious about dating for a while now.

"Girlfriend, you are not getting any younger and neither are the forty-year-old men who are finally ready to settle down and start a family with you," he says at least once a week. "You'd better snag you one before you miss out and end up waiting around for someone your age to finally be ready to commit. And that could be a while, Trudaloo. Boys these days can't be bothered to stop whoring themselves out all over town until they're at least thirty-seven. Trust me. If I weren't gay to the marrow of my rainbow-colored bones, I would have nothing to do with men. They're so entitled and obnoxious and have zero consideration for those of us who are ready to couple up and snuggle on the couch every Friday night in our mid-twenties."

Usually, at this point, the speech is briefly

interrupted by a dramatic sigh or a full-on collapse onto the fainting couch in the corner of the office, if he's having an especially challenging dating week. "I need someone to snuggle with, Trudy," he'll continue. "I'm becoming like one of those Russian orphans, the ones who weren't touched for years and failed to thrive. I am failing to thrive, woman! You have to help me find a boyfriend. Keep your nose to the ground and report all eligible gay men to me, and I'll do the same with the straight ones for you. With a little teamwork, we'll both be living happily ever after by next Christmas."

Of course, he's been saying the same thing since two Christmases ago, and so far, neither of us has a steady date, let alone a true significant other.

I hate to get Bradford excited for nothing but letting him think I'm personally interested in the Stafford brothers will ensure I get all the dirt the internet has to offer.

Rising from Sterling's chair and placing the phone back where it was when I entered, I do one final circle of the office, looking for other clues. But there's nothing personal on the built-in bookshelves or the small shelf filled with plants by the window. Even the books are generic classics, all with the same brown leather covers. There's nothing that reveals anything about Sterling's personal taste in novels or hints at whether he's Forrest or Barrick.

"Barrick, I'm guessing," I murmur aloud as I stare out the office window, watching the tall, powerful form of my mystery man cross from the smaller barn close to the house to the larger one down the hill, where the horses are stabled.

It's a hard, unyielding name, one that might grow a little boy into a man like this, one who keeps his cards glued to his chest and guards his secrets so fiercely he withheld from me both his first *and* last names.

But I know some of his secrets now, and soon I'll know more.

I also know his pain, and I feel for him. So much. I'm an orphan, too, after all. I know what that's like, but losing a sibling is different. It's something that shouldn't happen until you're at least sixty or seventy years old.

That's why I was willing to put myself in a situation like this one for my sister. If there's anything I can do to keep her alive and give her a new lease on life, I'll do it. Even if it's frightening in more ways than one.

Sterling's clear desire to control me is scary, yes...but how much I enjoy it?

That's even scarier.

I'll have to tread carefully and avoid getting in too deep with Sterling before I know the facts about who he is and what he really wants.

He wants to master you, use you for sexual pleasure, fuck you, and discard you, psycho. No matter what Bradford finds out, you won't be getting in deep with this man. You'll be servicing him and going on your merry way.

Right again, inner voice.

Though I choose to take its strident warnings as a positive reminder rather than a negative one. I *will* go on my merry way. I won't let this experience scar me, let alone destroy me. I will do what I came here to do, fulfill this bargain, and return to my life happy and proud that I did everything I could possibly do to save my sister.

And every time I wear this coat, I will think of what a goddamned ballsy-as-hell badass I am. Just like that pirate queen I wanted to be when I was growing up. A pirate queen would totally sell her hymen for half a million dollars. Not only that, she would do her best to enjoy as much of the experience as possible.

Moral quandaries, guilt, and shame are for

landlubbers. On the sea, we play by different rules.

Closing the office door behind me, I square my shoulders as I head for the front door, humming a sea shanty beneath my breath.

CHAPTER SEVEN

Sterling

I knew she was going to be beautiful in the clothes I picked out for her—I have excellent taste and a knack for dressing women which my ex-wife found delightful until she decided it was irritating and part of my "ruthlessly controlling nature."

But I didn't expect this.

Striding across the browning fall grass in tight pants that make her long legs seem even longer and that vibrant coat that makes her hair look even more like flame, she's...heart-stopping. Breathtaking. More beautiful than that night in the museum or all dressed up for the highest bidder.

Still, the compliment on the tip of my tongue dies as she gets closer. There's a hint of swagger in her walk and a bold light in her eyes that wasn't there before. My prey clearly realizes how fetching she looks and is, as my young interns say, "feeling herself."

And I can't have that.

I want her to enjoy our afternoon as a brief respite from my sexual torment, yes, but I don't want her too confident, let alone cocky —no matter how attractive I find the crooked grin on her face as she stops beside me in the wide door to the barn and props a hand on her hip.

"Do the clothes meet with your approval, m'lord?" she asks.

I fight a smile. "Sir when we're in the bedroom; Sterling the rest of the time, please. I haven't been given a title yet."

Her grin widens. "Really? Yet? So, you have connections in the old country, then? An in with the royal family? I thought only actors and rock stars got to be knighted, not financial wizards."

"Most knighted Americans were philanthropists of some kind," I say. "And they're only honorary knights. The queen isn't our head of state, so they aren't allowed to use 'sir' before their names."

"Interesting." She nods, before adding in a pointed voice, "And a bit of a letdown. If you don't get to be Sir Whatever Your First Name is Sterling, what's the point, right?"

"Correct," I say, my eyes narrowing on hers. "I will tell you my first name before we part ways, Trudy, if you still want to know it."

"But not now?" she asks, still with that edge in her tone that makes it seem she has an ace up her sleeve. "I mean, you know mine. It only seems fair that you grant me the same courtesy."

I wonder if she somehow managed to pry my name out of Harlow but dismiss the thought immediately. Harlow understands that I'm fiercely private and knows better than to gossip about her employer. So maybe Trudy took advantage of my offer to use the landline and called someone to do her digging for her in the absence of cell service or the internet available only on my laptop.

My laptop...

I realize my mistake and silently curse myself for it. I was so thrown by seeing Harlow and Trudy chummy in the kitchen I didn't think before I invited Trudy into my office.

She's caught me in a lie and is clearly feeling sassy about it.

But that's fine. She can feel as sassy as she

pleases. And she can sic her fiercest Google operatives on me if she wishes, as well.

She won't find out much beyond my name, age, where I went to school, and the company at which I'm currently head of trading algorithm research and development. I pay to have the web scrubbed of my more private information. Even the news of my divorce, which is a matter of public record, is buried several search pages in.

Still, the more I can keep her isolated from people inclined to help her without flat-out forbidding her to use the phone, the better. I don't want to be accused of holding her prisoner or scare her into running away before I've accomplished my goal. And the best thing I can do to prevent that is to appease at least some of her curiosity.

"Barrick," I say, stepping closer, until she tilts her chin up to hold my gaze. "My name is Barrick."

Her brows lift but she doesn't really look surprised. "Barrick Sterling. That's unique. Is it a family name?"

"Yes. From Scottish ancestors," I say, not correcting her assumption that Sterling is my last name.

My mother was a Sterling before she was married. She gave all three of her children her maiden name as a middle name as a compromise with my father, who refused to hyphenate his last name when they were married. The Staffords had more money and clout than the Sterlings, and he found the hyphenating trend "asinine and impractical."

"Thank you," she says in a softer voice. "For trusting me with that, Barrick."

"Call me Barrick again and I'll pull down those fetching pants and tan your lily-white ass," I say pleasantly.

She purses her lips, seemingly fighting a smile. "You've threatened to spank me so often that after I got dressed, I went searching for your secret spanking room."

I arch a brow. "Did you find it?"

She shakes her head. "Not yet."

"And you won't," I say, leaning down to brush my lips across her cheek before I whisper in her ear, "Because I don't require a special room, princess. I could spank you in any room in that house or anywhere on my land and no one would lift a finger to stop me. I am king here. Remember that the next time you're feeling sassy."

Her breath rushes out, warm on my neck as she whispers, "Yes, sir. Mr. Sterling, sir."

I pull back far enough to meet her gaze and shake my head the barest bit. "This isn't a game, Miss Potter. You will be receiving a spanking before we part company. With an attitude like that, it's only a matter of time."

"An attitude like what, sir?" she asks, blinking innocent eyes up at me that I'm not buying for a second.

I cluck my tongue. "Keep it up, little girl, and you'll learn how hot your ass can burn sooner rather than later." I motion toward the shadowed interior of the barn, needing to get her on a horse before all this talk tempts me to toss her over my shoulder, carry her back to her room, and start her education in the pleasures and perils of erotic punishment right now. "Shall we ride?"

She nods, seeming to make an attempt to keep her smirking and sass to a minimum. "Yes, please. I'm really looking forward to it. Your property is beautiful and the clothes you picked out are stunning and perfect. Thank you so much. I appreciate your generosity."

"You're welcome," I say gruffly, her graciousness making me feel like a beast for being so fucking eager to turn her over my knee.

Reminding myself that spankings are the least of the punishments I have planned for this woman, I lead her to the back of the barn, where my groomsman has already saddled the horses I selected earlier.

I thank and dismiss him before motioning to the slightly smaller mare with the golden coat. "I know you've ridden before, but I wasn't sure how long it had been. Honey's patient and responds to gentle cues."

"So, I won't have to dig my heels into her sides a dozen times?" Trudy grins up at the animal, stroking the horse's face and throat before she coos, "That's wonderful. I hate feeling like I'm kicking an innocent creature in the guts. Thank you in advance for being such a good girl, Honey."

The words on her lips instantly get me hard, sending images of her naked and spread out on the bed before me, ready to obey my every command, pulsing through my head. She was so fucking sexy last night, so innocent but eager to learn, to serve, to pleasure me and take her pleasure in return.

On impulse, I reach out, threading my fingers into her hair at the base of her neck and making a fist. I pull her closer, not missing the soft gasp that escapes her lips or the way her eyes go dark as I bend my face to hers.

"And thank you in advance for being a good girl, princess," I whisper inches from her lips. "Do as you're told this afternoon and I'll make sure you get a reward when we get home."

"A handful of carrots?" she asks in a husky voice that makes me even harder.

"If that's what you'd like," I murmur, playing along as I brush my mouth softly over hers. "Is that what you'd like, Trudy?"

"No, sir," she whispers, her arms going lightly around my waist. "I think I'd like something a little dirtier than carrots."

"Good," I growl beneath my breath. "Because the only thing better than you in these beautiful clothes is you out of them. Do you require assistance mounting your horse?"

Her eyes glitter up at me as I release my hold on her hair. "Um, no, I don't think so."

"Is something funny?"

She shakes her head. "Nope."

"I see," I say, nodding slowly. "So, you aren't laughing at the phrase 'mount your horse,' like a twelve-year-old?"

She lets out a soft snort that is oddly and powerfully cute. "It wasn't just the phrase; it was the *way* you said it." She furrows her brow and drops her voice. "Do you require assistance mounting your horse? Like you were asking me if I was wearing panties. It was the tone, Sterling. Tone is important."

"Are you?" I ask, casting a glance down to her lower half. "Wearing panties?"

She smiles and bobs a shoulder as she reaches for her horse's reins. "I can't remember. Guess you'll just have to wait and see for yourself."

And I will.

But I see a lot of other things first.

I see Trudy, pink-cheeked and grinning as we race our horses across the hayfield to the creek on the other side. I see her laughing with saucer-wide eyes as she takes her boots off to wade in the freezing cold brook, insisting it's good luck to get your feet in water in a new place, even if you have to put them at risk of frostbite to do so.

I see the wonder in her expression as I take her to my secret picnic spot at the highest point on the property, the one that gives a nearly three-hundred-and-sixty-degree view of the softly rolling hills, and the contentment in her features after our meal, when we're lying side by side on the blanket, watching the clouds roll by across a bright blue sky.

But even more important than what I see, is what I feel.

I'm relaxed with her. Relaxed and happy. She doesn't feel like a stranger. She feels like a friend, one I lost touch with and wish I hadn't now that I remember how easy it is to be with her.

How natural and...unusual at the same time.

I've had female friends and female lovers but never both in one person. Even with Celia, sex was the only place we deeply connected for a long time, and I wouldn't say we were ever friends. We were cordial companions, two icy rivers so snug in our individual beds that we never overflowed our banks and truly came together, no matter how many nights we slept side by side.

But with Trudy...

I can already tell how it would be with us if this were more than business or revenge. We would be easy together. Easy and electric.

She doesn't just make me smile far more than I have in years; she makes me burn. Every time her hand brushes mine as we reach for a grape in the bowl between us, my nerve endings dance and my cock perks up in hopes his services will soon be required. I want her even more than I did the night before because I like her more than I did the night before.

In less than twenty-four hours she's already under my skin, charming me no matter how I try to fight it. And wonder of wonders, she seems charmed by me as well. Even when I've clearly irritated her, she seems to feel the pull between us as powerfully as I do.

Just your luck, the bitter voice in my head pipes up as we head back toward the barn. *Drop half a million dollars on a plan that's doomed to fail and start falling for the one woman you can't have.*

My chest tightens. It's true.

I can't have her, even if I'm right and she feels this pull between us. Her stepbrother murdered my mother and sister. I will *never* be a part of Connor Potter's family or sit across from him at holiday dinners. I would rather die first. Or be sent to prison for murdering Connor—assuming I get caught.

"Is it too late for tea?" Trudy asks, arching a brow. "I know you're not supposed to have caffeine so close to bedtime, but I think I might need a jolt of something to keep me awake through dinner."

"You're exhausted by trying to keep up with me? Is that what you're saying?"

"Maybe." She smiles, that easy, relaxed smile that made its first appearance while we were lying on the blanket and that makes her even more beautiful. Her heart is in that smile and this woman's heart is clearly every bit as stunning as it looks on paper.

When I first read that she ran a charity for deaf children and spent her spare time volunteering at senior living centers and raising money for various cancer research funds, I rolled my eyes so hard it made my head ache.

I've been surrounded by virtue-signaling rich women my entire life. And yes, they do good things for people, but they do those good things for an excuse to buy designer dresses and throw lavish fundraising parties. Or to appeal to the wealthy men on the marriage market looking to marry a younger, hotter version of their fundraising, gala-throwing mothers.

But Trudy's not like that. She's just a good person who's trying to do good things with her money and her life. A good, brave person who is going to make this process harder for me than I ever imagined possible.

"Yes," I say, swallowing the regret rising in my throat. "You can have tea. I'll have Harlow send some up to your room while you're getting changed."

"Thank you," she says, smiling. "And thank you for the wonderful afternoon."

"My pleasure," I say, truthfully, as her

horse pulls ahead of mine on the trail, eager to get back to barn and the oats waiting there.

The sunset glow catches Trudy's hair as we move out of the trees, making it burn like a homing beacon.

Or a lighthouse, guiding the way safely to shore.

Nothing about this situation is safe, for either of us, of course, but it *is* a stroke of luck, I realize. The inner voice is wrong. The fact that Trudy and I are so drawn to each other won't make this harder. It will make it easier, *if* I'm willing to adapt to the shifting situation.

I excel at adapting. It's the reason I've been the head of my department since I was barely twenty-eight. I'm always the first to see when an algorithm is failing and how to shift our formula to adjust to changing times and market patterns.

There's no reason I can't do the same thing here.

As we enter the barn, I release the old plan. It isn't hard. Subjecting Trudy to a mixture of kindness, abuse, and sexual frustration before dumping her on Connor's front door—freshly deflowered and hopefully pregnant with a baby who would remind them both for the rest of their lives of the man who treated her terribly

—was a decent plan. But making Trudy fall madly in love with me, making her think she's found her happily ever after, and *then* rejecting and abandoning her, will be even worse.

She'll doubt her own sanity, her ability to judge a lover's sincerity and when it's safe to trust. That kind of betrayal will wreck her more thoroughly than a pattern of abuse ever will. I won't break her mind, I'll break her heart and let it shatter the rest of her for me.

And if I destroy myself while I'm at it…

Well, that's a price I'm willing to pay.

Once we've given the horses to the groom, who leads them into the back of the barn to unsaddle and brush them before their dinner, I pull her into my arms beside the door leading outside. I brace my hands on either side of her shoulders and gaze into her eyes, dropping my guard and letting what I feel for her rise to the surface, hoping I haven't grown too rigid and reserved for my emotions to show on my face.

My fears are instantly put to rest. Trudy's eyes widen in surprise but just as quickly warm and soften.

"I enjoy your company," I whisper, my voice rough.

"I enjoy yours, too," she says. "Very much."

"I would like to kiss you," I confess. "May I?"

Pleasure blooms on her features. "Yes. Please."

I kiss her softly at first, my lips teasing against hers, the barest brush of hot skin against hotter, softer skin. Despite the cool day, her mouth is burning up, warming my tongue as I part her lips and explore her sweetness. She moans and presses closer, clinging to me as I deepen the connection, kissing her like I can't get enough of her mouth.

And I can't.

I crave this girl like I haven't craved anyone or anything in so long—maybe ever.

It's going to be hellish to hurt her, let alone break her.

But I've been in hell since her brother killed my sister. This is where I live now, and this is what I do. I'm a devil this sweet girl should run from as fast as her long legs can carry her.

Instead, she wraps them around my waist as I lift her into the air and press her back against the smooth wood beside the door, kissing her until she's breathless and trembling. She wobbles as I set her back on her feet. I offer my arm, and she clings to it for support.

"Thanks," she says with a soft laugh. "Guess that 'weak in the knees' thing isn't a myth after all." She bites her lip, hesitating a beat before she adds, "Thanks for asking permission. The big bad billionaire who takes what he wants is sexy but...that's nice some-times, too."

"It is," I agree, leading her out of the barn and toward the house, wondering how "nice" she'll find this memory when she looks back on it later, through the lens of heartbreak and betrayal.

CHAPTER EIGHT

Trudy

It wasn't a date; it was part of a half-a-million-dollar business deal.

And just because he asked for permission once doesn't mean he won't go back to being a jerk who complains about how bad you are at sex later tonight.

I remind myself of these very true and logical things at least a hundred times in the shower. And then I get out to find tea waiting on a tray on the bench at the end of the bed, as promised.

I thought Sterling might have forgotten—that kiss in the barn was hot enough to wipe most other thoughts from my mind—but he didn't.

The tea is there in a darling china pot, with a tiny jar of honey and a little pitcher of milk beside it. I pour myself a cup, a goofy smile spreading across my face that I know spells trouble. I can't let myself enjoy this man any more than I have already, and I certainly can't let myself develop feelings for him. That would be breathlessly stupid.

Pretty Woman was a fun Cinderella story but things like that don't happen in real life. The john doesn't fall in love with his whore.

I flinch at the word.

A whore.

That's what I am. It's shocking and mortifying but it's also...not nearly as bad as I was expecting it to be. I'm enjoying most of my time with Sterling—in bed and out of it—and I'd rather kiss him than any man I've ever kissed before.

But maybe that's just my subconscious, deciding to make the best of the situation since I'm trapped here anyway. Maybe I'm already developing Stockholm syndrome and falling for my captor, though I'm pretty sure anything with the word "syndrome" in it is something that takes longer than a day to happen.

I can't believe it's only been a day.

When I descend the stairs to meet Sterling for dinner, my heart squeezes when I spot him on the far side of the room, his broad shoulders highlighted by the last of the sunset light. And then he turns, as if he's sensed me behind him though I haven't made a sound.

Our eyes meet. Potential energy fills the air. And then...he smiles, and my heart thumps even harder.

"Hey," I say, feeling shy and happy and scared to death all at once. I could fall for this man, I realize. It would be the biggest mistake I've ever made, but it could happen. I might not be able to stop it from happening, not if he keeps looking at me like I'm the best thing he's seen in ages and like he's hated the hour we spent apart as much as I did.

"Hello," he murmurs, his warm gaze travelling down to take in my outfit.

I motion toward the simple, rather shapeless green sweaterdress. "Sorry. I didn't have anything fancier. I didn't realize I'd be dressing for dinner when I packed. I thought I'd mostly be...undressing."

His lips hook up on one side. "You look beautiful, but you're right, I think we can do better. We'll go into the village tomorrow. There are several upscale clothing stores that cater to the gentleman farmers of the area. You can pick out whatever you like. Or I could just order what I think will suit you best and have the items delivered."

I nod. "That's probably for the best. You have excellent taste."

"I do," he agrees in a matter-of-fact way that makes me laugh.

"So humble," I tease.

"False modesty is tedious," he says, motioning toward the table and the place settings laid out close together at one corner. "I had Harlow move you closer. It feels silly to eat at opposite ends and shout at each other through the entire meal."

"Agreed," I say, moving toward the chair he's pulled out for me.

"And this way I can fondle your knee under the table while we eat," he murmurs as he tucks the chair gently into the backs of my legs.

I glance over my shoulder, my breath catching as I realize how close his face is to mine. "You can fondle more than my knee, if you like."

His gaze heats. "I have your permission?"

"My enthusiastic permission," I whisper, my nipples tightening as he brushes his mouth across mine.

"And what about later?" he says, kissing me again between the words. "Do I have your permission to not ask permission? I want to do bad things to you, beautiful."

I tilt my head back, welcoming the feel of his lips trailing down my throat. "What kind of bad things?"

"The kind where I get you so turned on that you're begging me to get you off, but I make you suffer, instead. I want to make you want me so much it hurts, princess." He drags his knuckles across my tight nipple through my dress, making things low in my body clench. "And then I want to be the one who makes the hurt go away."

A part of me wants to ask if that means we're going to have sex tonight, but the other part of me doesn't want to give him any ideas. Insanely, I'm not ready for this to be over just yet. If he takes my virginity, I'll have no reason to stay. And I want to stay, at least a little longer, long enough to make more sexy memories with this man—and to see him in Alpha Asshole mode again.

I could use that reminder that it's best that this...whatever-this-is has an expiration date.

Making a mental note to write down every obnoxious, aggravating, or abusive thing he does from now on, I lift a hand to his face, resting cool fingers on his cheek as I say, "You have my permission to do all of those things. But if you touch my nipple again, I can't promise to behave myself long enough to let you eat."

He pulls back, his lips twisting. "Is that right? What would you do? Tackle me on the dining room floor?"

"Maybe. My nipples are...sensitive."

"I've noticed." He settles into the seat catty-corner from mine, a spark in his gaze I don't understand until he adds, "But if your sweet ass gets out of that chair before we're finished eating and you've been excused, you're going to get that spanking you're after, princess."

Biting my lip, I nod. "I'll consider myself warned. But why princess?"

He settles his napkin into his lap just as Harlow pushes through the door leading down into the kitchen carrying two bowls of something that smells divine. "You don't think it fits?"

"Thank you," I tell Harlow as she sets my bowl in front of me, waiting for her to deliver Sterling's and start back across the room before I answer the question. "No, I don't. Do you? You're the wealthy, polished one around here. I'm the girl who sold her body for money. Not very princessy in my book."

"I don't know," he says, lifting his spoon and dipping it into the thick orange broth, tipping it away from himself, not toward, like the well-heeled man he is. "I imagine a good number of princesses sold their bodies for money. Or bartered them for one reason or another. Royal marriages weren't often love matches and whoever had the money had the power."

"Men had the power," I counter. "At least mostly. I know there are a few queens who held their own, but they were the exception not the rule." I dip my own spoon into the soup. "So, I guess you're right. The nickname does fit. Like princesses of old, I'm at the mercy of the wealthy man who acquired me at auction."

"And you like it," he challenges, watching me over the edge of his spoon. "More than you ever imagined you would."

I let the sage and butternut squash–flavored delight slide down my throat, silently warning myself that dangerous games have dangerous prizes. But when my mouth is empty again, I can't stop myself from whispering, "My panties are wet pretty much constantly, so...yes. I do like it, sir."

He sets his spoon down and deliberately places both hands flat on the table on either side of his plate. He then takes a breath and lets it out slowly before he asks in a calm voice that's at odds with the heat burning in his eyes, "Can you wait an hour for dinner?"

I set my spoon down and nod, my heart already racing. "Yes. I can."

"Good," he says. "Go upstairs. My room is to the left, last door at the end of the hall. I'll let Harlow know that we'll have food sent up later and be up to join you in a moment."

I scoot my chair back, but stop before I stand when he adds, "And, Trudy?"

"Yes?" I whisper.

"Clothes off, face down on the bed, arms extended in front of you," he rumbles. "You're going to pay a price for getting my dick too hard to enjoy my appetizer."

I fight a smile. "Yes, sir."

He shakes his head, his eyes glittering. "What a little brat you are, princess. You can't wait to be punished. Can you?"

"I don't know. I've never been punished before," I say, before I confess in a softer voice, "But no, I'm not scared. I'm...excited."

"And wet?" he prompts.

"So wet," I say, giving him what he clearly wants, loving that hearing how turned on I am is what drives him crazy. "My panties are soaked. They've been that way all day. I want you to touch me so badly."

"Then hurry upstairs, little girl," he

rumbles, the hunger in his gaze making my nipples even tighter, until they sting with the need to be touched, kissed, licked, and sucked. "I'm going to make all your pain and pleasure dreams come true."

Pulse throbbing in my throat, I stand, fighting the urge to slide into his lap and crush my lips to his. I don't know if I can wait the five or ten minutes it will take for him to join me upstairs.

I need him now, like an addict needs a fix.

The thought reminds me of my sister, of why I'm here and how soon this will be over. I'm on borrowed time with Sterling and that time will run out soon. Maybe tonight if he decides he's had enough foreplay and is ready for the main event.

I use the sobering thought to cool my blood long enough to hurry up the stairs and down the hall to his room. But by the time I'm naked and facedown on his heavenly-smelling, soft-as-an-angel's-cloud bed, I'm trembling again.

I need his touch so badly that I'm not worried about my impending "punishment." I'll take whatever he needs to dish out, secure in the knowledge that pleasure awaits at the end of the discomfort.

He won't actually hurt me, after all. I don't

know much about BDSM, but I know that's not how it works. That's why submissives have safe words, to let their Doms know they've pushed things too far.

When I hear the door open behind me a few minutes later, I ask, "What's my safe word? Just in case?"

He doesn't answer, but I hear the door snick closed and then the rustle of what sounds like clothes being removed. A light sweat breaks out along the valley of my spine even as my sex throbs harder, deeper, until I can feel the hunger pulsing all the way into my core.

I'm about to ask again when the mattress dips and suddenly Sterling is on top of me, his hands braced on either side of my breasts as he hovers over my nude form, close enough for me to feel the heat of his body but not the brush of his skin against mine.

A moment later his breath stirs the hair at my neck as he whispers, "Why do you need a safe word, princess? Don't you trust me?"

"I do," I say, starting to shiver again. "I'm just not great with pain."

"It won't be that kind of pain," he says, before he asks, "Are you cold? Should I turn up the heat?"

"No. I'm just..." I swallow and push aside

the embarrassment clutching at my throat. If I only have one more night with Sterling, I refuse to spend it feeling self-conscious. "I just want you so much. My skin feels like it's starving."

"Mine, too," he says, the mixture of wonder and need in his tone making my soul light up. "You are so damned beautiful like this. I can smell how wet you are, princess, and it's driving me fucking crazy. It's going to take every ounce of willpower I have not to take you tonight. I want to feel that hot, slick pussy locked around my cock so badly. Want to bury myself so deep inside you."

My breath rushes out and my back arches in an instinctive plea for him to touch me, to mount me, to do whatever has to be done to relieve the almost panicked lust building beneath my skin.

"Do you want my hands on you, baby?" he asks, his lips dragging across my shoulder blade. "Do you want me to make you come?"

"Yes," I breathe, arching even higher, until my ass lifts into the air, brushing against his hips and the thick, throbbing erection behind his fly.

But before I can whisper how much I love feeling him hard for me, he's pushed my hips back to the mattress and delivered a sharp swat to my right butt cheek.

I gasp, a turned-on sound that becomes a moan as he grips my stinging flesh in one big hand and squeezes it hard, sending more bruising pleasure pulsing up my spine. "Sorry, princess. You've been bad. Punishment first, then pleasure. Now spread your legs, I want to watch my pussy swell while I spank you."

The sound of him claiming my body as his own as he swats my other cheek with his free hand makes my head spin. But I cling to rational thought for a few more seconds and ask, "Safe word? What is it?"

He answers me with another stinging slap to my ass and then he shoves my thighs wide and drives a finger into where I'm wet. I cry out in gratitude for the penetration I'm craving so badly, all thoughts of safe words evaporating as he shows me how good it can feel to be bad.

I've never been this hard, not even in the observation room at Persephone's Closet, when blindfolded Trudy was naked and at my mercy and rubbing all over my cock.

That was hot—hot as fucking hell—but this...

The flames building between us as I spank her sweet ass, leaving red handprints all over her pale skin, while she wiggles and juices all over my finger is explosive. I'm burning up and taking a beat to quickly dispose of my clothes before returning my attention to her hot ass and hotter pussy does nothing to cool me down.

"Please, oh, please," she begs, wiggling on my finger as I squeeze her bottom tight in one hand, taking the edge off the sting before I slap her again. "Oh, Sterling, God, please!"

"Please, what, little girl?" I ask, cock leaking as she scrambles at the covers with clawed hands. "What do you want? Use your words."

"I want more," she says, panting as she adds with a moan, "Please, give me more."

"More of this?" I spank her again, three times in rapid succession, making her cry out and the muscles in her back tighten as she arches her spine, granting me easier access to her pussy. I reward her with two fingers pumped deep into her dripping channel. "Or more of this?"

"Yes, yes," she pants, writhing under me now, so turned on she's wild with it. Sweat is breaking out between her shoulder blades and on instinct I bend, licking the beads from her soft skin, groaning as her salt and flower taste floods my mouth.

Even her sweat is delicious, but not as delicious as her cunt.

And just like that, I need her on my mouth, need her arousal coating my tongue so badly I can't wait another fucking second.

I scoot lower on the mattress, gripping her hips and flipping her over onto her back. I grip her swollen ass cheeks in both hands and pull her to my mouth like a man desperate for water after days lost in the desert, moaning with pleasure as my tongue drives deep into her heat. She tastes like the ocean, primal and fierce and demanding my respect, my reverence and worship.

"Feels so good," she says, her fingers threading into my hair as she presses me tighter to her sex. "God, Sterling, it feels so good. I love your mouth. I love your mouth on me, in me. You make me crazy."

I groan my agreement against her clit, making her buck sharply into my lips. I hum again and she chants, "Yes, oh yes, please. *That*, keeping doing that."

Happy to obey my bossy little virgin who took her punishment like a goddess, I intensify the connection between us, fusing my mouth to her sweetness, fucking her with my tongue as I vibrate her clit with long, deep groans. Soon, she's squirming so frantically beneath me that I have to grip her hips hard, holding her prisoner as I drive toward the inevitable conclusion.

I will have her orgasm. At least one, but hopefully more.

Her pleasure is fucking addictive, making me so hard that by the time she finally tumbles over, flooding my mouth with more of her salty juices, I'm humping the mattress like a damned teenager.

I surge over her, crushing my lips to hers as I finish her off with my fingers, drawing out her orgasm as my balls drag heavy between my legs, demanding I replace my fingers with my cock.

I'm so far gone, so desperate to be inside her, that I might have forgotten that penetrating her means losing her and made a serious fucking mistake, but before that happens, she takes matters into her own hands.

Her fingers wrap around my shaft, pumping hard as she pants between kisses, "So good. You make me feel so good. Want to make you feel good, too. Need to make you come, Sterling. Need it so bad."

"Fuck, princess," I gasp, clenching my jaw as I pull away from her lips to watch her owning my dick with urgent strokes. "Just like that. Jerk me hard. Fuck, yes. Harder."

She obeys, squeezing my shaft until it almost hurts, but it doesn't because this is what I need from her. I need wild and urgent and fierce. I need her labored breath echoing mine as she takes me closer to the edge.

Closer, closer, until flashes of light are exploding around the edges of my vision and

I'm balancing on the razor's edge. I bite the inside of my cheek hard enough to send pain flashing through my jaw, praying the discomfort will be enough to help me hold on for just a few more seconds.

"Fuck your tits," I manage to grit out. "Need to fuck your tits. Push them together for me."

She releases my cock with a moan, her hands immediately moving to press her breasts closer together at the center of her chest.

Rising over her and straddling her ribs, I grip the base of my cock and order, 'Tighter, baby. Make a tight fuck hole for me. Tight like your sweet little cunt."

Her teeth dig into her bottom lip as she obeys, smashing her gorgeous, erect nipples so close together I could take them both in my mouth at the same time.

So, I do. I bend down, lips closing around the twin buds and suckling hard and deep. She cries out and squirms under me, making my suffering cock leak all over my hand as I grip my erection hard, fighting my release.

Finally, when she's moaning and clawing at my shoulders, I release her nipples with a slick popping sound and reposition myself, guiding the head of my suffering dick to the base of the channel she's created with her breasts.

I push into the sweat-slick softness, cursing as I glide all the way through until the head of my dick emerges on the other side, just inches from her chin. I thread my fingers into her hair, making a fist and holding on tight as I lock my gaze on hers. "So fucking sexy. You're so sexy, princess. Fuck, I'm going to come so hard."

"Yes," she says, her lips parted and her eyes glittering with desire as I thrust between her breasts again. "Yes, I want you to come. I want to drive you crazy. Make you feel the way you make me feel."

"What do I make you feel, beautiful?" I ask, my mouth falling open as I near the edge. "Tell me." I thrust faster, pumping between the tits she's holding so tight together for me, fire gathering at the base of my spine.

"You make me feel savage," she says, her eyes staying locked on mine as I tighten my grip on her hair. "Wild and shameless and so good. So good, Sterling, so good."

"Fuck, baby," I choke out, my pace growing erratic as I start to unravel. "Gonna come. Can I come on you, princess? Want to come on you so fucking bad."

"Yes," she says, lifting her chest and

pressing her tits even closer. "Come on me. Come all over me. I need to feel you. Need it so bad."

I come with a roar, thrusting forward between her breasts one last time as semen explodes from my tip in thick, powerful jets. I clench my jaw and groan deep in my chest, memorizing the way she parts her lips and closes her eyes, accepting the baptism of my come as it hits her cheek and then her throat before sliding down her chest. She truly seems to enjoy it as much as I enjoyed feeling her juices running over my lips and face.

Afterwards, I fall forward, bracing myself on the headboard as I catch my breath and wait for my bones to feel steady again.

When I've regained enough control to trust I won't crush her as I roll away, I swing my leg over her ribs and settle onto the mattress beside her, propping myself up on one arm as she turns to face me.

Her cheeks are pink and her eyes shining as she whispers, "That was...really good."

"Incredible," I agree, my gaze raking down to the come on her chest. "But you seem to have gotten a little...messy at some point."

Her brow furrows as she asks, "Really? Messy? In what way?"

My lips curve. "Someone seems to have

come all over you, darling. I think there might be semen in your hair."

She widens her eyes in feigned surprise. "Really? In my hair? How...wonderful."

I laugh softly. "I doubt you'll think so if it has a chance to get sticky. I hear it can be a bear to get out. You should jump in the shower."

"I will not jump in the shower," she says with a happy sigh. "I will slowly ooze toward the shower as soon as I can feel my legs again."

Still grinning, I squeeze her thigh. "How about I carry you to the shower? Or, better yet, run you a bath and carry you to that?"

Her smile as she says, "Yes, please. That would be very nice," is sweet and heart-breaking at the same time.

She's so damned trusting, so good and innocent, that I can't help whispering, "You should be more careful, princess. With that smile. Only share it with men who deserve it."

She reaches up, touching gentle fingers to my cheek. "Well, I happen to think the man who just made me come harder than I ever have after giving me my first spanking—which I found delicious, by the way—deserves to be smiled at. I mean, I let you come all over my face again, Sterling. If that's okay, I think smiling is probably okay, too."

"Point taken." I turn, kissing her palm as her fingertips press lightly into my face.

Connection pulses between us, drawing me to her, making my throat tight with guilt. But I push it away and try to relish the sensation instead. The fastest way to get Trudy to fall for me is to let myself fall, too. To let myself relish every second with her and to let her see how much I crave her company, her body, and that beautiful, oh-so-vulnerable grin.

"I'll be back," I promise, sliding off the bed before I say, "I'm going to draw a warm bath, not a hot one. If the water's too hot, it might sting your tender areas."

She watches me back toward the master bath, hunger in her eyes. "Will you be joining me in this bath?"

"If you'd like," I say, unable to resist though a part of me warns that it's dangerous to be naked with her anymore tonight. I want her too much. The longer I'm close to her like this, the better the chances that I'm going to fuck her and ruin everything.

I can't let her go yet. Not until I finish what I've started, and I've made her love me enough now to ensure she hates me for the rest of her life—and that her stepbrother does, too.

She nods loosely and sighs, stretching her arms over her head. "Yes, I would like. I hear soap feels good on a person's nipples."

"You want me to wash your tits for you?" I ask, just the thought making my cock start to perk up again.

Trudy shakes her head. "No, I want to wash yours. I want to rub the soap on your nipples and circle each one with my finger until you're begging me to touch you in other places."

I smirk. "Sounds fun, but fair warning, my nipples aren't nearly as sensitive as yours, baby. You're going to have your work cut out for you."

"I always thought I'd hate being called baby or little girl. Things like that. Things that I'm supposed to find infantilizing or demeaning," she muses, her gaze dragging down my chest to my swelling cock. Her tongue sweeps across her lip, making my balls feel heavier before her eyes flick back to mine. "But I don't. When you say them, I like it. A lot."

"Good," I say, my voice rough. "I like calling you those things."

"What should I call you?" she asks. "What pet names do you like in bed?"

"Sterling. Or sir. Those are good enough for me."

Her lips turn down in a cute little pout that makes me want to kiss her again. But at this point, what doesn't? "Those are good, but what about when you've done a very good job and I want to be sweet to you? I need something softer than 'sir.'"

"I'm not a soft man," I say, arching a wry brow. "Which I'm sure you've noticed by now."

She hums beneath her breath, her gaze heating as she nods. "Yes, I have. You get hard again very quickly. It's most impressive, pumpkin."

I scowl—instantly and fiercely—and she laughs.

"Sugar?" she asks, giggling again as I fake a gag. "You're right, that's too sweet. You need something with a little edge to it. How about...captain? As in 'captain, oh my captain'? I've always thought that Whitman poem was sexy."

"It's about Abraham Lincoln," I say, folding my arms over my chest.

She nods, her gaze brightening. "I know.

He's my favorite president. And a sexy historical figure, don't you think?"

I arch a brow. "Do I think Lincoln was sexy?"

"Yes," she chirps, grabbing the pillow behind her and propping it under her head. "I mean, sure he was supposed to be tall and gangly and obviously wasn't perfect, but he stepped up for our country in a major way at a pivotal point in history." She glances down at her chest, frowning before she looks back to me. "The come is congealing, captain, my captain. Better get that bathwater running before we have a paper-mache-level cleanup situation on our hands."

I shake my head, fighting a smile as I murmur, "Bossy little virgin."

She wrinkles her nose. "You like it. You know you do. I can see it written all over your face. And your cock." She drops her voice to a dramatic whisper. "Don't look now, but you're hard again, captain. I think that means you really want to go get dirty with me in the bath, but as a bossy little virgin, I can't be sure."

I laugh, a real laugh, one that hasn't rattled through my chest in too long, and cross back to the bed, scooping a giggling Trudy into my arms before aiming us both toward the bathroom.

We're still in the tub—making each other moan with erotic soap torture—when Harlow knocks on the door to deliver our dinner.

I call for her to leave it on the table by the window and return to making Trudy come on my hand as I grind against her ass from behind. I come like that, exploding beneath the water at the same moment Trudy arches into my fingers with a cry, like a teenager making out with a cute girl for the first time.

But Trudy is so much more than cute and all woman, a fact she proves as she turns in the water, straddling me as she says, "I finally get it. What all the fuss about sex is about. Thank you so much." She kisses my cheek and I wrap my arms tighter around her slim form.

"My pleasure, princess," I murmur.

And it is and will continue to be my pleasure, until the day this thing we're building together comes crashing down.

CHAPTER TEN

Trudy

The next morning, I wake up alone in Sterling's bed.

I know instantly that he isn't there, even before I open my eyes. I can sense his absence the same way I can sense his presence. A room just feels more full, more alive, when Sterling's in it.

"And smells way better," I mumble in a sleep-rough voice as I roll over to bury my face in his pillow, inhaling the sweet and smoky cedar scent of his shampoo deep into my soul.

I'm still there, huffing his bedding like a total weirdo when a deep voice from the doorway says, "I hope I'm not interrupting something."

I roll back over, my cheeks heating with

embarrassment as I brush my hair from my face. "Nope. I'm good. How did you sleep?" I see the tray he's holding and my jaw drops. "Is that for me?"

"It is. I thought you might like some coffee and fruit before breakfast." As he crosses the room, he adds in a cheerful voice, "And I slept terribly. There was a beautiful woman in my bed who kept rubbing her ass all over my cock, making it very difficult not to wake her up and finish what we started."

I sit up, propping myself against the headboard as he settles the tray across my lap. "Sorry about that," I say, butterflies swarming in my stomach as he braces a hand on the bed behind me and leans down to kiss my cheek.

"Don't be," he whispers into my ear, making me shiver. "I told you, I enjoy foreplay. Even when it grows a little…"

"Tedious?" I supply, my breath catching as he cups my breast through the t-shirt of his I pulled on to sleep in.

"More like torturous," he corrects, rubbing his thumb softly over my nipple before he pulls away, leaving me aching for his hand between my legs as he crosses the room and disappears into his massive walk-in closet. "Which is why I'm taking you out for break-fast," he calls from inside. "Maybe that way, we'll actually stay put long enough to eat. When you're done with your coffee and fruit, get dressed and meet me downstairs in my office. There's a message in my voicemail that you should hear before I delete it."

The coffee I just cream-and-sugared clatters back into its saucer. "A message? From whom?" Bradford hardly ever checks his messages on the weekend, but maybe I got lucky.

Or unlucky, if he has terrible news to report about Sterling.

I bite the inside of my lip, anxiety swelling in my chest as I mentally replay what I said to Bradford and fret about what sort of incriminating message he might have left. I should have warned him that I wasn't on a private line, and it wasn't safe to leave revealing messages, dammit!

But when Sterling emerges from his closet, now wearing a gorgeous light gray motorcycle-style jacket over his blue t-shirt and black jeans, he says, "It's your sister."

I press a hand to my chest. "Oh God, no. What's wrong? Did she miss the plane and not get checked in to rehab? I knew I should have called her a few hours before to remind her that—"

"No, she's fine. She's safe at the facility. It's

you she's worried about, but her ex-husband won't be able to hurt you while you're here." He motions to my tray. "You're safe. Enjoy your coffee, get dressed, and when you're ready you can listen to the message and call Millie to assure her everything's fine."

I sit back against the headboard and collect my coffee, something still not sitting right with me. I sip the delicious liquid as I watch Sterling cross to the door.

It isn't until he's nearly out in the hall that I realize what's nagging at me and call out, "But how did she know where I was?" He turns back to me, and I add, "I didn't give her this number. I didn't have it when we texted. I didn't even tell her your name or that I was with a man."

"I contacted the facility and had them add my number to your sister's emergency contact list. Just in case she needed to reach you."

My jaw drops and sputtering noises emerge from my lips, so many questions surging into my head at once that I can't choose one to ask first.

Sterling leans against the doorframe, crossing his arms as he adds in an almost bored voice, "I'm not the type of man who buys a woman without knowing why she's selling herself, Trudy. Or making damned sure she's doing it out of her own free will. Persephone's Closet has an exceptional reputation, but human trafficking is a serious problem and no operation that does business outside the law should be taken at face value." He pauses, his brows rising up his forehead as he adds, "I'd say the same for all businesses, actually. Always best to do your due diligence."

Saving my thoughts on Sterling's trust issues until later, I demand, "But how did you find out that Millie was in trouble let alone where she was staying? Medical records are confidential. And there are hundreds of rehab facilities in the country."

Sterling continues to look bored. "Yes, there are. But there are only a handful that cater to wealthy people with enhanced security concerns. Your sister's marital and drug problems are a matter of public record. Looking at her life history compared to yours, it quickly became clear that she was most likely the reason you were suddenly in urgent need of capital. Though your charity's finances aren't in the best shape. You seem to be on the upswing now, but it was a mistake to mingle personal funds with your nonprofit."

I wrap my arms around my ribs, holding myself together. "You lied to me. You pretended to know almost nothing about me, when in reality, you knew my entire life history and had your nose ten inches into my business."

He arches a brow. "My nose is large, granted, but not that large. An inch in your business, perhaps. Two inches at most."

I scowl at him, not in the mood to be charmed by his dry sense of humor. "Meanwhile, you didn't even want to tell me your name. Your *name*. Don't you see how messed up that is?"

"But I did tell you my name and I made it possible for your sister to reach you in an emergency. If you'd like to continue to berate me for that, I'll be down in my office answering email." He reaches for the door handle, adding in a terse voice, "And yes, I lied about having internet access, too. Because I value my privacy and didn't want a woman I bought at a virginity auction posting pictures of herself in my home to social media. Your phone will be checked before you leave, by the way. And you'll be expected to sign a nondisclosure agreement about your time here."

"Because you're so important and the only person who matters?" I scoff. "Maybe I'll want to check *your* phone, too. And have *you* sign legal paperwork."

"If that's the case, then you should arrange to be the person with power in your business relationships from now on," he says, his tone sharpening. "I bought *you*, Trudy, not the other way around. And you should be on your knees thanking me for that. The other men in that room wouldn't have given a damn if your sister lived or died or if you experienced pleasure while in their company. In fact, I'm certain some of them would have enjoyed your suffering, that inflicting pain on an untried young woman was the entire point." He moves to shut the door but opens it again almost immediately. "And I've been very good to you so far. Very, very good. Don't make me regret it."

"Or what?" I ask, setting the tray on the bedside table and swinging my legs out from under the covers to stand on the soft carpet beside the bed. "You'll debase me, insult me, and jerk off all over my face because I'm not good at sucking cock? Please, Sterling, remind me again of what a catch you are. Because I—"

My words end in a frightened yipping sound as he surges across the room. Before I can even think of running—let alone decide where to run *to*—his hand is around my throat, and I'm pinned to the wall behind me.

He brings his face a breath away from mine and whispers, "I'm sorry."

The words are so at odds with the domineering way he's touching me that I have trouble processing them. "Wh-what?"

"I said that I was sorry," he repeats, his grip on my neck tightening ever so slightly, making me realize how careful he's actually being with me.

I'm immobilized but he isn't hurting me or choking me. He's just...controlling me, silently letting me know who's boss even as he apologizes.

"I shouldn't have treated you that way," he continues. "You're not bad at sucking cock. You're quite good at it actually and...I wasn't prepared for that. Or for the things I felt when you touched me. That's what made me angry, my lack of control over my emotions. I took that anger out on you, but I shouldn't have, and I'm sorry."

I look up at him, blinking as he shifts back far enough for me to pull his face into focus. He looks angry, but also confused. And, most of all, sincere.

"You were mad because you...like me?" I ask, voice shaking as I bounce between irritation and disbelief and a tiny flicker of excitement that sparks to life in my chest.

He frowns. "For some reason...yes. I do."

I arch a wry brow as I add in a flat voice, "Please, stop. The flattery...it's too much."

His lips twitch but he doesn't smile. "You're nothing like the women I usually date. But that night at the museum... I couldn't get it out of my head, even though I knew the chances of running into you again were slim, even if I went to every opening night exhibit for the next year. When I saw you at Persephone's, it felt like a sign. That I was meant to have you and get you out of my system."

"Like a virus?" I murmur, getting sucked into his gruff, sexy voice—and his story—despite myself.

This time his features do soften and one edge of his full mouth lilts up. "Yes. Very much like a virus. One that arrived at an inconvenient time and seems to be much harder to shake than I first assumed."

I swallow, nerve endings fizzing as my throat works against his palm. "I know the feeling. You're more...infectious than I expected you to be, too." I bite my lip, that heavy, hungry feeling spreading through my core as I add, "So you aren't going to strangle me?"

"No," he says, his gaze drifting to my mouth. "Not today. But I would very much like to pin you to the floor like this while I make you come on my hand."

"You can't make me come, I'm too mad," I say.

"Want to bet?" he asks, his voice so deep now that I can feel it buzzing against my erect nipples. "If I can make you come on my hand in the next ten minutes, you forgive me for snooping into your past and we start fresh today with no ugly secrets between us."

"And if you can't?" I ask, even though my panties are already wet, and my body clearly has no interest in holding a grudge against this man.

"Then you can take the money and go without honoring the rest of our bargain," he says in a softer voice. "And you never have to see my face again."

The thought sends pain flashing through my bones.

I don't want to say goodbye to him yet, no matter how violated I feel.

Seeming to sense my weakening resolve, Sterling leans in, pressing his cheek to mine as he whispers in my ear, "Come on, princess. Let me show you how sorry I am."

A beat later, his hand is on my belly beneath the t-shirt, sliding down the front of my panties. His voice goes gravelly as his fingers slide through where I'm already wet and swollen. "So fucking sorry."

I gasp as he pushes two fingers inside my body, shoving in and up with a force that makes me keenly aware of the fact that I've just been invaded, but is also insanely hot.

The barely contained violence in his touch, his voice as he adds, "I don't want you to leave, Trudy," makes me tremble and cling to his shoulders.

A moment later, he's guided me to the ground, his fingers fucking me with sharp, insistent strokes as he pins me to the ground by my throat. "I want you to stay, and I want to get you off a hundred times, a thousand," he says, his mouth claiming mine, swallowing the turned-on sounds emerging from my lips. "I want you to crave my touch like you crave sleep and air. I want you to beg me to fuck you. I want to be the first man to take you, the only man to take you."

Panting beneath him as my orgasm swells inside me like a rocket building the power to launch into space, I whimper, "Yes, please. Now. I want you now."

"Without a condom?" he asks, the knuckle of his thumb rubbing against my clit as his fingers continue to demand my surrender. "Because that's how I want you, little girl. I want you bare on my cock. Fuck, I want it so bad, I want to bury myself in you so deep and come right at the end of you. I want to fill you until you overflow."

The words should chill my blood in my veins and banish my lust like a blast of artic air sweeping into the room.

Instead, they make me wild, feral.

"Yes, please yes." I shove at his shoulders, pushing hard until he pulls his fingers from my body long enough for me to drag his jacket down his arms. I rake my nails down his back through his shirt before I jerk the fabric from his pants and drive my hands up and under the fabric, too hungry for his bare skin to mess with the buttons at the front. "Now. Please, now."

"You could get pregnant," he warns, but he doesn't fight me as I transfer my attention to the front of his pants, fumbling open the button and zipper with shaking hands. "I mean it, Trudy. I won't pull out. I'll come with my balls wedged into the crack of your ass I'll be so fucking deep inside you."

His words make me moan. My head spins and my now empty pussy clenches frantically around its own emptiness.

I'm beyond words now, beyond any thought except that I need him inside me, doing every wicked, irresponsible thing he just said.

Some small, logical part of me warns that having a child with this man would be breathlessly stupid, maybe even dangerous, but that voice is soft and weak compared to the primal feminine need roaring through my veins.

I want this man—*my* man.

I want him to take me bare and fill me with his release. I want to cover him with my scent, mark him as off-limits to all other women who would dare to get close to what's mine. I want to merge with him, lose myself in him, and the chance that we might make a baby while we're tangled up in each other only makes the moment when I pull his throbbing erection from his pants that much hotter.

He curses as I stroke him up and down. "Fuck, little girl. I'm not going to be able to stop soon. I'm going to take you, Trudy, without protection. Going to bury my dick so damned deep inside you. Tell me to stop."

"Don't stop," I demand, pushing his pants down over his ass. I grip his thick glute muscles in my hands and whisper against his lips, "I want to hold on to you like this when you're inside me. I want to feel your muscles working while you fuck me."

The words have the desired effect. They

apparently trip the primal switch in Sterling, too, reducing him to grunts and swiftly drawn breaths as he jerks the t-shirt over my head and drags my panties down my thighs.

A few seconds later, his own clothes are gone and he's kneeling between my thighs, naked and glorious. He fists the base of his cock in his hand, reminding me how obscenely large he is.

Even in his big, wide palm, his cock looks massive.

And angry.

He's so swollen that his shaft is flushed a deep red, nearly purple at the tip. He's leaking pre-come, making the head glisten as he tips his cock down. He looks up, catching my gaze as he says through a clenched jaw, "Last chance, baby. Last chance before I'm inside you, taking what's mine."

I lift my knees and spread my legs wider, reaching for him as I say, "Take it. Take *me*. Now."

He lengthens himself over me, pushing my torso back to the ground as he kisses me hard. I feel the burning head of his erection brush against where I'm slick and ready and my heart skips a beat. Excitement and a hint of fear streak through me like lightning. And then he's starting to push inside, demanding entrance, insisting I take what I've asked for.

My nipples bead into tingling points and fresh heat rushes between my legs as I brace myself for the pain I know is coming. No matter how much I want him, no matter how hungry my body is for his, losing your virginity is painful. Or at least a little uncomfortable.

All my girlfriends have said so, even the ones who had gentle, attentive lovers who did their best to make the first time as satisfying for them as possible.

For a moment fear becomes my dominant emotion, sending a blaring alarm sound ringing through my ears.

Then Sterling curses and moves away from me so fast I'm left sputtering on the floor, and I realize the alarm isn't in my head. It's coming from Sterling's phone. Still naked, he stands, his jacket in hand. He pulls the cell from inside one pocket and lifts it to his ear to bark, "What is it? Where's the breach?"

He listens to the voice droning on the other end of the line for a few seconds, his eyes narrowing before he snaps, "What? You're sure?"

The other voice murmurs again and Sterling's free hand curls into a fist. "Yes, that's the one I called you about earlier. Good work. And no, don't confront him. He won't be able to reach the house in the next fifteen minutes. Just help the police when they arrive. Give them a ride to the location in the four-wheeler." His gaze fixes on my face. "And keep me posted. I want to know the second they have him in custody."

I sit up, grabbing the t-shirt I slept in and using it to cover my breasts. "What is it?" I ask when Sterling ends the call. "Someone trespassing on your land?"

"Not just someone," he says, his voice cold. "Your brother-in-law. I think you'd better come listen to that message from your sister. Now."

CHAPTER ELEVEN

Sterling

I want to kill him. Dead.

I want to wrap my hands around his throat and watch the light fade from his eyes.

I've never experienced murderous urges toward someone I haven't met before, but this man not only wants to hurt Trudy, but he was also able to track her here to my property. That shouldn't have been possible.

My name isn't on this deed. The estate is owned by one of my subsidiary companies. And even if it were, he shouldn't have been able to connect me to Trudy. The people at Persephone's Closet are known for their discretion and I was careful to ensure no one saw me entering or leaving their building that day.

I suppose he could have bribed someone there to tell him who purchased Trudy, but that raises the question of how he could have possibly known that Trudy was planning to sell her virginity.

"Did you tell your sister what you were planning to do at Persephone's Closet?" I ask a pale Trudy as she finishes listening to her sister's message and sets the phone back in its cradle with a trembling hand.

She shakes her head as she sags back into my desk chair. "God, no. No. I would never —*will* never. She would feel so guilty. I don't want that for her. I just want her to focus on her recovery and staying healthy for the baby."

"That's what I thought," I say, pacing slowly back and forth in front of the bookshelves. "And you didn't tell anyone else where you were or who you were with?"

"No," she says, hesitating a second before she adds, "Actually, that's not true. I called into my office yesterday and left a message for one of my colleagues. I asked him to dig up any gossip he could find on Barrick or Forrest Sterling Stafford. I wasn't sure which one you were at that point." Her shoulders hunch closer to her ears. "Sorry. I lied a little. Like you did about the internet. I'm assuming that's how your cell is working, by the way? It's connected to your Wi-Fi?"

"Yes." I rearrange my expression as best I can before I continue, not wanting her to know how much she's surprised me. "How did you ferret out that information without cell service of your own?"

"I snooped through your desk," she says, regret tightening her forehead. "I found your sister's funeral program. It had both your and your brother's name on it. I'm so sorry. For your loss and for invading your privacy. That's not something I would usually even consider. I was just...nervous."

I cross to the desk. "It's all right. It's my fault. I was being a withholding, controlling bastard."

"You do like control," she says, a smile in her voice that fades as she adds, "But I seriously doubt Bradford, the colleague I left the message for, has even checked his voicemail yet. He usually doesn't on weekends. And I was careful during the call. I didn't tell him I was with you. I said I was at a cabin by myself unplugging for the week. I asked him to look into you and your brother as potential donors, that's it. I kept the tone light." She drags a hand through her hair with a sigh. "And even if he somehow read between the lines and was worried, he wouldn't tell Harrison who I was with. I've warned my staff about him, and Bradford and I are close outside of work. He knows how awful Harrison has been to my sister." She rolls her eyes. "And me. He's always hated me. Since the beginning."

I circle around the desk and lean against the heavy wood beside her. "Why? So far you seem uniquely likable."

She cocks her head. "I might be flattered if you didn't sound disgusted."

My lips twitch. She's perceptive as hell, this woman. It only confirms my gut take that the only way to fool her is to fool myself while I'm at it. Trudy might be innocent and have led a relatedly sheltered life, but she's good at reading people.

Even cagey, guarded people like me.

"I find being likable a waste of time and energy," I confess. "But I enjoy your likability. As long as you don't have to work too hard for it, it's...fine."

Her brows shoot up as she huffs out a soft laugh. "Fine?"

"Good," I amend. "It's good. I'm sure people appreciate that trait in a woman who raises money for charity."

She huffs again. "Right. Well, thanks for that rousing endorsement. I think most people would agree with you, at least about the likable part, but not Harrison. He hated me from the first night Millie brought him over to my place for dinner."

"You're a horrible cook. Makes sense. I figured there had to be something wrong with you."

She smiles and shakes her head. "No, I'm actually an amazing cook. And that night I made slow-cooked spareribs just for Harrison because Millie said they were his favorite. But he spent the entire night complaining about my father's will. He thought Connor and I had received more than our fair share and was pretty pissed about it."

I grunt softly, careful not to let mention of my enemy's name cause a blip in my cool façade. "And your sister? Was she angry too?"

Trudy shakes her head. "No. Not at all. I got a little more money than she did, but not that much, and it was for my charity. She knew that and she was proud of me."

"And your brother?" I ask as casually as possible.

"Stepbrother," Trudy corrects, distaste flashing across her features for a moment before she composes herself and adds, "And no, Millie wasn't angry with him. At least not about being given control of our dad's business. Millie has always hated Connor, but it has nothing to do with that."

"What does it have to do with?"

She shrugs uncomfortably. "Oh, you know...family stuff. They're both type A personalities and clashed from day one. And Connor was always...odd. And abrasive. Millie didn't have a lot of patience for that, and Connor doesn't have patience for anyone, so..."

"Even you?" I turn it into a joke as I grin and add, "Miss Likeable?"

She laughs, but it's a tight, strained sound. "No, he likes me. Mostly, anyway. I'm one of the only people he can tolerate for more than an hour at a time. So, I get the honor of attending boring work parties with him whenever he's between girlfriends and he's almost always between girlfriends." She frowns. "But yeah...Millie wasn't upset with him about the money and later she told me she couldn't remember telling Harrison anything about the will. And granted, my sister has an ongoing drug problem, and doesn't always remember everything she's said when she was under the influence, but that always stuck with me. That Harrison might have dug up the will on his own. It made me worry that he was after Millie for the wrong reasons."

"For her money," I supply. A part of me wants to circle back around to her stepbrother and pump her for more information, but I don't want to make her suspicious. And she's confirmed what my gut and my private investigators uncovered—that Trudy is the only person Connor actually cares for—was correct. That's enough for now. "Did you talk to your sister about your concerns?"

She shakes her head and slumps lower in the chair. "No, I... I did that once, when we were younger, and it didn't go well. Millie shut me out completely for a few months and I just..." She sighs. "I couldn't take it. She's the only real family I have left, the only person I know will always love me no matter what."

"She probably wouldn't have listened anyway," I say, hoping it gives her at least a little comfort. "People are never more unreasonable than when they're falling in love."

Trudy's wry smile tugs at her lips again. "Likeable and love. Two L-words you don't care for. Are there any others? What about libation? Because I could use a drink even if it is nine a.m." The words seem to remind her of something. She sits up straighter and points to the phone. "That message from Millie. She called at eight p.m. our time yesterday, five p.m. on the West Coast. And when she called,

Harrison was outside the rehab gates demanding to be let in to see her."

"Which means he flew across the country and found his way here in about twelve hours. Impressive."

"Crazy," she mutters, fear creeping into her eyes. "And why is he here? What does he really want? Millie said he threatened to kill me to get back at her for leaving him but that's insane. Even for Harrison. I can't believe he would really do it."

"Hopefully we'll have answers soon." I squint toward the window. It's an overcast morning, and the fall leaves stand out even more brilliantly against the slate gray sky. It looks so peaceful out there, but it isn't. Just a few acres away, a man is about to be handcuffed and hauled off my property.

It might even be happening right now.

I glance at my watch, frowning as I see how much time has passed. But Chris at the gatehouse would have called if there were any news to share. He's a former Marine and counterintelligence agent and one of the most dependable members of my security staff. He was also able to get a positive ID on Harrison within just a few minutes of running the security footage through facial recognition software.

It makes me wonder…

"Does Harrison have a criminal record?"

Trudy draws her knees into her chest and hugs them close, making her look almost childlike balled up in the center of my big chair. "I don't think so." She winces self-consciously. "I never thought to look, honestly. I'm so bad at things like that. Bradford says my suspicious radar is broken. I take people at face value more than I probably should."

That's absolutely true.

Guilt swells inside me, bigger and more insistent than before, crowding my lungs until it's hard to breathe. But thankfully, my cell rings a beat later, providing a much-needed distraction. It's Chris at the gatehouse.

"Is the situation under control?" I ask as I answer.

Chris exhales a frustrated breath. "No, sir. The police couldn't find him. He must have heard the sirens while they were driving up and made a run for it. The last security footage we have of him, he was running along the back gate, close to the old homestead. I sent Ben to check it out and he said it looked like they guy had gone under. There was a bunch of loose dirt near a hole at the base of the chain link."

"Find him," I say. "Have Ben stay at the gatehouse and call in Teddy and Rex for backup. The police had their chance. Now we'll take care of this ourselves."

"Will do," Chris says. "I'll make a citizen's arrest and call them to come pick up the package. Would you like me to send someone up there to keep an eye on the house? And your guest?"

"No, thank you," I say. "I'll keep an eye on her until she's packed. We'll be leaving soon."

Trudy's eyes widen, and when I end the call, she says, "Where are we going?"

"Somewhere your deranged brother-in-law won't be able to find you." I motion toward the landline. "If you have anyone to call, you should do so now. We'll be in the air most of the afternoon."

Her eyes stretch even wider. "The air? Will we be able to get tickets that fast?"

I smile and reach out to brush her hair from her forehead. "I have a private jet, princess. We don't have to worry about tickets."

She blinks faster as she sets her feet back on the floor. "Well, then... Another reason *your* nickname should be princess, not mine. I mean, seriously? A private jet? Isn't that a little excessive?"

"You can complain about my excessive habits on the way to somewhere warm and sunny, with a beach. Or cold with enough snowfall for skiing. Which would you prefer?" I ask, warming to this plan.

What better way to ramp up the romance and speed the falling-in-love process than with a spur-of-the-moment vacation? We'll be alone, relaxed, and focused exclusively on enjoying each other and Trudy will feel less like a captive in my home and more like my guest.

Or...my girlfriend.

The thought gives me another idea. "We could rent a honeymoon suite somewhere, check in under assumed names, make it really difficult for anyone to find us. My ex and I skipped our honeymoon, so I can't say for sure, but I've heard they're enjoyable."

"You skipped your honeymoon?" she asks, her brow furrowing. "Why?"

"We were both very devoted to our jobs at the time."

"So? You still make time for a honeymoon. Time to celebrate your devotion to each other. That's important. Skipping it probably wasn't the best way to start your marriage."

"Obviously," I state dryly. "As we're divorced now. But thank you for the feedback.

Though I would prefer your feedback on our choice of vacation destination. If you don't choose soon, I'll decide on my own."

She stands, bringing her eyes nearly level with mine in my position leaned against the desk. "Why?"

"What?" I frown. "Why should we avoid my other properties until your brother-in-law is taken into custody? Primarily because I don't know how he found you here or how he knew you were with me in the first place. Until we sort out where the information leak is coming from, lying low in a place I've never visited before seems like the best way to keep you safe."

Her gaze softens. "No, I mean...why are you so determined to keep me safe? We almost..." Her cheeks flush but her gaze doesn't waver from mine. "We almost sealed the deal this morning, Sterling. You could take me upstairs, finish what we started, and send me on my way. Once that happens, I won't be your problem anymore. Harrison is after me. This has nothing to do with you."

I clench my jaw, choosing my next words carefully. I can't rush this. If my transformation from unfeeling captor to smitten suitor happens too quickly, she'll be suspicious.

After a moment, I shrug and say, "I'm not

ready to move forward with that just yet. I require more foreplay."

Her eyes narrow. "More foreplay?"

I nod. "Yes. But, as I stated before, you're free to go before we consummate our arrangement. You'll be safer with me, but...that's your choice. Though if you choose to leave, I *will* be sending one of my guards to watch over you until Harrison is captured. If Chris is able to track him down today, that could be as early as this evening. But it could be longer, and I won't take no for an answer regarding your safety, so don't even try to convince me it's acceptable for you to head out on your own. That would be a waste of time and breath."

She shakes her head, a bemused smile lilting across her face. "That's very bossy. And very kind."

I frown. "It's not kind. It's decent. There's a difference."

Her smile widens. "Yes, Grumpy, I know there is. But sending one of your staff to watch over a stranger you hardly know *is* kind, not just decent. And nothing you say can convince me otherwise." She leans closer, adding in a confidential tone, "But here's the thing...I don't have my passport."

The relief that washes through me is ridiculous, but I can't help it.

I tip my chin down, softening my voice to match hers. "Then it's a good thing we live in a country where there are both warm beaches and snowy mountains just a few hours' flight away. Where would you like to go, little girl? Choose your adventure."

Her chin jerks up and worry thins her lips. "That reminds me... Could we stop by a pharmacy on the way to the airport? I think condoms of various kinds and the morning after pill would be a wise investment. Just in case."

My jaw tightens and my cock thickens behind my fly as memories of our near-miss on my bedroom floor flood my mind. "Various kinds?" I murmur, holding her gaze as awareness pulses in the air between us.

She nods slowly, even as her face drifts closer to mine. "They have condoms for women now, right? I could get some of those, too."

"I'm not sure they're as effective as condoms for men," I say, covering her hand with mine and pinning it firmly to the desk. "I believe they can be more difficult to position correctly."

"They'll be more effective than nothing at

all," she says. "And I can put one in before I get overwhelmed by sex magic and decide you wanting to come inside me is the sexiest thing I've ever heard and that condoms are stupid."

I fight a smile. "Condoms are stupid. And I would argue that you saying you want to feel my ass muscles work while I fuck you is the sexiest thing ever. And I would have worked you, princess. Worked you as hard and deep as you needed me to. I promise you that."

"Stop." Her hand squirms lightly beneath mine, but I simply pin her wiggling digits more firmly to the wood, summoning a soft, sexy sigh from her lips. "Seriously. We should talk about the weather. Or world hunger or something. No more sex talk until we're properly equipped. No matter how good it would feel in the moment, we don't want to bring an innocent life into...whatever hot mess this is."

My brows lift. "I take offense to that, Miss Potter. I'm an ice-cold mess, not a hot one, and don't you forget it. Now tell me where you want to vacation or I'm going to assume you want me to make the decision for you."

She grins and lifts her chin, offering me her lips. "I've always wanted to go to Key West. Ride in an air boat. See alligators. Drink beer on the beach while a bearded man sings about his lost shaker of salt. But if that's too pedestrian for you, I understand."

"Not at all," I assure her. "Assuming you don't mind adding a five-star resort with a swimming pool and a golf course to that list."

She wrinkles her nose. "Dammit. You're a golfer."

"I am. Always loved the game."

She sighs. "Rats. But I knew there had to be something wrong with you, too. Other than the obvious things, of course."

Again, I find myself fighting a smile, then wondering why I'm fighting so hard. This woman amuses the hell out of me, a man who hasn't smiled more than once or twice a week in years.

Might as well let her know it.

I relax, letting my grin take over as I murmur, "Of course. The obvious things. You'll have to tell me all about those on the plane. Maybe you can help me clean up my act a little before we get home."

"Maybe," she says, playing up the doubt in her voice. "But you may be too old and set in your ways at this point." Her eyes dance as she adds, "What are you? Forty-five? Fifty?"

I grin wider. "Not quite, but still a good deal older than you, brat."

"That isn't an answer. *And* that's one of

your less than perfect qualities. You're cagey and unwilling to answer even basic questions."

"I'm a private person."

"You're pathological," she says pleasantly. "Just tell me how old you are, Barrick."

"I'm thirty-one, Trudy. And you're cruising for another spanking."

She laughs and lifts her eyes to the ceiling before they slide down to meet mine. "Oh, no. Not another spanking. Whatever will I do?" Her fingers squirm again, and I shift my grip, locking my fingers around her thin wrist. Her eyes darken and my erection presses more insistently against my zipper as she says, "I can't wait to be on a beach with you. I'm going to get a book at the airport and pretend to read it, but I'll actually be staring at you over the pages and ogling your chest. Your chest is very nice."

"Your chest is also very nice," I say, drawing her closer. "As are your lips."

"Barrick?" she whispers, something in her tone making me pause with my mouth just inches away from hers.

"Yes?"

"Can we try it more than once? I know you only paid for once and that was the agreement but I..." She pulls in a breath before she adds, "I'm going to want to do it more than once. *Need* to do it more than once."

I transfer my hands to her hips, dragging her in front of me and urging her thighs apart. I pull her forward, cupping her ass and pinning her to my swollen cock, loving the way she gasps and instantly rocks her pelvis forward to intensify the contact.

I curl my fingers around the back of her neck and whisper against her lips, "I will fuck you as many times as you want me to fuck you, princess. I will take you slow and sweet and hard and fast and every way in between. Up against the wall, in the shower, in the ocean, on a blanket on a darkened beach while I crush my hand over your mouth so no one can hear you come. By the time we fly back, you'll be so satisfied you'll sleep like a baby the entire flight home."

"I'll hold you to that," she says, and then she kisses me, taking the lead for the first time.

Her fingers twine into my hair as her tongue parts my lips to stroke against mine, building the heat already burning through my veins. I fist a hand in the loose linen pants she threw on to come downstairs and rock between her legs, fucking her slow and easy through our clothes, shocked when an orgasm begins to gather low in my body.

I haven't come like this since I was a teenager, sneaking out behind the girls' campus to roll around in the fall leaves on the far side of the quarry, the place our keepers never dared to check.

My first time was with a senior named Melissa who was very understanding when I lost control in my pants while we were dry humping on the ground, long before we got close to the main event. I was only fifteen, after all, a sophomore, and was able to rally again quickly.

And my premature ejaculation was probably for the best.

Once I rolled on the condom and pushed inside my senior sex tutor, I was able to hold on for five whole minutes—instead of the two pumps I likely would have lasted straight out of the gate—giving Melissa time to teach me how to finger her clit while we fucked. Watching her come was even more satisfying than coming myself. The power I felt as this older, more experienced girl panted beneath me, her face twisting into a mask of pleasure as I got her off, was intoxicating.

By the second time we met up, I was already accomplished at giving her what she wanted. By the third time, I was confident enough to try a few new tricks I'd learned from watching feminist porn, the kind that shows what it really takes to satisfy a woman, not the parody of pleasure made for men.

A couple of the guys in the dorm caught me watching one night and started calling me "Lezzie" in honor of my taste for watching older lesbians fuck under poor lighting. Their mockery lasted a few weeks before it became clear whatever I was doing was intensely successful with the female population.

Melissa wasn't interested in being exclusive, and it was never more than friendly fucking between us. She didn't care if I branched out to practice my newfound skills with other girls.

And the other girls...

Well, they couldn't get enough of what I had to offer.

I graduated high school knowing more about women's bodies than most grown men and with a confidence in my skills that has never wavered. I might not know how to sustain a healthy, long-term relationship—and I'm as chilly and emotionally detached as the rest of the men in my WASP family tree—but I'm good at this. Good at making women moan and melt and want more of what I give them in the bedroom.

But as Trudy straddles my hips more fully, her feet coming off the ground as we kiss like it might be our last chance to touch another human being for years, I don't feel confident or in control. For the first time in longer than I can remember, I'm off-balance, taken by surprise by the ferocity of her hunger and the intensity of my own reaction to it.

Maybe it's because we were interrupted so close to completion upstairs. Maybe it's that I haven't been buried deep inside a woman in far too long. Or maybe it's just Trudy, her sweetness and honesty and this unexpected intensity that has me off my game and out of the driver's seat. But within a few seconds of her grinding frantically against my erection, I'm past the point of no return.

I grip her ass hard in both hands, biting my lip to muffle my groan as I come in my pants just seconds before she cries out and begins to tremble and twitch on top of me. She clings to my shoulders, and I cling to her curves, both of us gasping, open-mouthed, for air.

She rests her forehead against mine, waiting until her breath slows before she whispers, "Did you…"

"Yes." I should probably be embarrassed but I'm too relieved to care. I needed something to take the edge off before I did something stupid like strip her naked and rush her first time.

I don't want to rush with her. I want to play with her, tease her, pleasure her to within an inch of her life and make sure she has the best "losing it" story possible to tell her friends.

Girls talk—I learned that early on as word of my skill set spread through the girls' campus—but women do, too. Giving Trudy a story that part of her will be dying to tell, even as another part of her laments how terribly our relationship ended, is just good revenge planning.

But it isn't vengeance on my mind as I kiss her cheek and confess, "First time since I was a teenager."

She smiles, her cheek plumping against my lips as she wraps her arms around my neck. "Because I drive you crazy?"

"Absolutely out of my mind," I answer honestly.

"Good," she says, hugging me closer. "You do the same to me. I can't wait to be with you, captain."

"Same, princess," I whisper, my heart at

war with itself as I wrap my arms around her and bury my face in the curve of her neck.

I could love her. I truly could, in a way I've never loved another woman before and probably never will. How could I? Once I've broken this sweet girl, I'll have proven beyond a shadow of a doubt that I'm a monster.

Just like Connor.

But sometimes it takes a monster to destroy a monster and I've lived long enough to know life and love are rarely easy and almost never fair. All I can do is give Trudy as much pleasure as possible before the pain and brace myself for the end when it comes.

Because it's going to be ugly.

No doubt about that.

CHAPTER TWELVE

Trudy

The next few hours are a whirlwind.

Sterling stays busy on the phone, arranging for the plane to be prepped and the pilot called in, while I shower, dress, and repack my small suitcase, leaving the riding coat hanging in the closet since I won't need it on the beach.

I finger the soft wool for a moment, silently hoping I'll be back to reclaim it or even get to wear it on another ride with Sterling. Then I remind myself that Sterling and I have an expiration date and firmly close the door.

But it feels different between us than it did before.

I feel close to him, connected. The way he clung to me after we made out in his office made my heart peek out from behind the bars I erected to protect it during this experience and stand, aching and hopeful, in the door to its cell, wondering if it might be safe to leave its cage behind.

And then I tiptoe downstairs to overhear Sterling rumbling to someone on the phone, insisting they, "Keep looking. See if you can pick up his trail. I don't care if it's a long shot, Chris. I need to know she's safe," and that's it.

I can't fight it anymore.

The bars around my heart crumble and suddenly I'm standing in the middle of the dining room, my hand pressed to my chest as it floods with emotion. I feel so many things at once that it's hard to name them all, but hope is definitely there.

So is lust and longing and affection and just plain old appreciation for this person who seems to truly care about my welfare. Maybe it's just base-level caring—most decent human beings don't want to see other humans viciously attacked or worse—but my gut insists this is something more.

That embrace we shared earlier wasn't casual or impersonal.

It was...intense.

Nearly as intense as the way my body responds as Sterling steps out of his office a moment later, spotting me in the dining room at the end of the hall, and barking, "What are you doing? Get back upstairs. Harlow's gone to fetch resort wear in town. You'll need to try on the swimsuits to see which ones fit."

"And which ones you like the best," I say, pretending my cells aren't humming just from the sexy way he leans against the doorframe.

"Obviously." He nods toward the stairs. "Go on. Get up there and get undressed. She should be back any moment and we only have an hour before we need to leave for the airport."

"So that means no stopping between suits to make out?" I arch a teasing brow, heart skipping a beat when he smiles again, without fighting it the way he usually does.

"No," he says, still grinning as he adds with a wink, "No matter how much you beg."

"How much *you* beg, you mean," I say, blood fizzing as I grip the handle on my suit-case and spin it around to head back the way I came.

"Leave it," Sterling says. "I'll carry it up for you when I come. It will give me something to do with my hands instead of touch you."

Excitement dumping into my veins at the thought that he needs help keeping his hands off me, I nod and give him a little salute. "Yes, captain."

THIRTY MINUTES LATER, I've tried on four gorgeous swimsuits and twice as many sundresses and breezy, floaty cover-ups and am feeling quite spoiled as Sterling insists I "pack everything," and then excuses himself to attend to his own bag, before he loses control and "rips that bikini off" of me with his teeth.

Fantasies about how incredible it would feel to be at the mercy of Sterling's teeth dancing through my head, I layer my brown cardigan from home over a new brown and white sundress and pair knee socks with my new leather riding boots, figuring I can swap them for sandals after we land in Key West.

I meet Sterling downstairs a few minutes later, where Wells is already loading our luggage into the back of the limo. Sterling stands beside the car, glaring at his cell, but his forehead smooths as I step outside.

"Perfect," he says, his gaze sweeping up and down my frame. "Though a hat would complete the look."

I smile. "If the finance thing doesn't work out long term, you could become a personal stylist." His stunned, slightly horrified expression makes me laugh. "You should see your face," I murmur. "Relax, Sterling, I'm not trying to threaten your masculinity. Lots of very manly men work as personal stylists."

His eyes narrow as he reaches to open the limo's back door. "Right. I was more offended by the inference that I might fail in my area of expertise but thank you for the reassurance. I'm not worried about my masculinity."

My brows lift as I move to stand in front of him, peering up into his handsome face. "No?"

"No." His gaze flicks from my eyes to my lips and back again before he smiles and nods toward the open door. "Get in, brat, and I'll remind you why you shouldn't doubt it, either."

And he does, all the way to the airport.

By the time we pull up to a sleek private jet parked at the end of the tarmac, my clothes are rumpled and my cheeks are flushed. I'm too embarrassed to look Wells in the eye as he opens the door for me. Sterling assured me the partition between the front and the back was soundproof, but like the few times I got caught sneaking in after curfew because I lost track of time while making out with my boyfriend, I'm sure my face betrays exactly what I've been up to.

I'm so focused on keeping my head down and smoothing my wild hair that I don't hear Sterling clearly the first time he murmurs something behind me.

I glance over my shoulder as I step into the front of the private jet and Sterling closes the hatch behind us. "What was that?"

"I said I'll be back to join you shortly after takeoff. I'm working on my takeoff and landing skills, but Trevor will do most of the flying." Sterling nods over my shoulder. "Do you think you'll be able to entertain yourself for twenty or thirty minutes alone?"

I turn back to the cabin, trying not to geek out too hard as I take in the cushy leather seats in the front of the plane—complete with a library of magazines tucked into a built-in basket on one side—and the couch and big screen in the back. Not to mention the bar area and what looks like a mini fridge and a small glass cabinet packed with snacks.

"I think I'll be just fine," I say, patting his arm. "I'm going to devour a fashion magazine and some chocolate if I can find some and be even deeper in bliss by the time you get back."

Smiling, he bends to kiss my cheek. "Sounds good. Chocolate's in the mini fridge.

I like my dark chocolate refrigerated and with caramel in the center."

I moan softly. "Stop. You can't get any hotter or it won't be fair."

"Fair to whom?" he asks. "The other men who will attempt to impress you after I'm gone? Because I'm not concerned about them, Trudy. In fact, I prefer not to imagine another man's hands on you. Ever." He squeezes my ass tight enough to make me yip before adding, "Make sure you're buckled up soon. It won't be long before we're taxiing."

And then he opens the small door leading into the cockpit and disappears before I have a chance to say anything about how...territorial he just sounded.

Those weren't the words of a man who's planning to drop me off at my apartment as soon as we return from our vacation. Those were the words of a man who feels possessive about his woman, a woman he doesn't want to share with other men—not now, or in the near future.

At least, I think that's what he sounded like. It would be so nice to be able to talk to a girlfriend—or Millie—about Sterling. But Millie wasn't allowed to come to the phone when I called the rehab, though they did promise to convey my message that I'm safe and watching my back. And my other girl-friends would make way too big a deal about me flying off to paradise with a stranger.

But there is one person I can try, assuming I finally have service.

Pulling my cell from my purse as I cross to the mini fridge, I let out a soft "huzzah" as I see bars and claim a very fancy caramel-filled chocolate bar moments later. Scrolling through my contacts, I find Bradford's cell number, the one I don't have memorized. I tap the contact and put my cell to my ear as I cross back to one of the plush seats.

I sink into the supple leather with a happy sigh that becomes another yip of surprise as Bradford answers on the second ring and shrieks, "Jesus Christ, I thought you were never going to get back to me, woman. Where the hell have you been? Your cell isn't ringing, you didn't leave a callback number, and what-ever number you were calling from was blocked."

"Sorry," I say with a nervous laugh as I pluck my dropped chocolate off the floor and buckle my seat belt. "I didn't realize it was blocked. What's up? Fair warning, I can't talk very long. I'm on a plane and we're taking off soon."

"A plane? To where? I thought you were

unplugging at a cabin upstate. Whatever," he says, pushing on before I can answer. "I need other answers first. Like how on earth you've lived your whole live as a high-society princess and have no idea who your enemies are."

Scowling, I stop trying to unwrap my chocolate with one hand and set it on the wide armrest instead. "What enemies?"

"The Sterling Staffords," he says, making my stomach clench. "Or more accurately, the plain old Staffords. Apparently, your families have been feuding for centuries. There's a rumor your great-great-something-grandfathers almost fought a duel over some mansion in Cape Ann that's still being valued at millions less than the surrounding properties because their family won't grant permission for yours to build a new road to your mansion through the land they own all around it."

I scowl so hard my head starts to ache. "What? I mean, I know the estate owns a property on Cape Ann, but—"

"And that's not all," Bradford cuts in. "Your grandmother spread a rumor about his grandmother that got her kicked out of polite society and one of his great-uncles got one of your great-aunts pregnant and then abandoned her at an illegal abortion clinic where she later died. And don't even get me started on all the really old news. Your families have literally been fucking each other over Game of Thrones-style for hundreds of years."

Heart leaping as the engine rumbles to life, I press a hand to my suddenly clammy forehead. "So, Barrick Sterling Stafford going out of his way to flirt with me would be a weird thing," I say, wishing I felt comfortable telling Bradford the whole truth.

But my pride won't allow it. I don't want the people I work with—or anyone else—to know I sold my virginity at an auction.

"Assuming he knows you're one of *those* Potters, yes, very," Bradford confirms. "But if you didn't tell him your last name, maybe—"

"I did tell him," I say, my pulse racing faster as the wheels on the plane begin to roll. "And he knows who my family is. I'm sure of it."

"Then you want to proceed with caution, honey," he says. "It could be a Romeo and Juliet thing, but it could also be some sort of sick vendetta on his part. Vengeance for what your family did to his family in the past or something."

"Romeo and Juliet died," I squeak, my mouth flooding with a sour taste as I reach for my seat belt. But it's too late to make a run for it, we're rolling faster now toward the runway.

"And I'm already on a plane with him, Brad-ford. A private jet allegedly headed to Key West from a small airfield near New Paltz. Though he could be taking me anywhere for all I know."

"Oh fuck," he says, the fear in his words hitting me like a punch to the gut. "Have you taken off yet? Can you get out and wait for me to come pick you up at the airport?"

"No, it's too late." I bite my lip, fighting the tears rising in my eyes. "Just like you always say, my suspicious radar is broken and now who knows what's going to happen."

"Let's think positively," he says, but I can tell the cheer in his voice is forced. "Maybe he doesn't know about the family feud, either, and running into you upstate was just a coin-cidence."

And maybe Sterling buying one of the Staffords' enemies at a virginity auction was a coincidence, too, but I seriously doubt it. This connection between our families makes an already odd situation even harder to believe.

And then there's how easily Sterling was able to find out where my sister was and his lies about the internet connection. He clearly knows a hell of a lot more about me than I know about him and wants to keep it that way.

Why would he want that unless he planned to use the disparity in our knowledge of each other to his advantage in some way?

To get me on a plane headed to an even more remote location than the one we just left, where no one will be able to hear me scream or know where I am, for example.

"I'll call you as soon as we land," I tell Bradford, raising my voice to be heard over the groan of the plane's acceleration for take-off. "Or tomorrow if I can't get to a phone right away and my cell isn't getting service. But if you don't hear from me by tomorrow afternoon, then—"

"I'll have the FBI all over this by night-fall," he assures me as the wheels lift off the runway, making my stomach lurch. "Don't worry, honey. And there's still a chance every-thing is fine. And if so, I want to be the first to congratulate you on landing that prime piece of man meat. Assuming he isn't a vengeful psychopath out to punish you for your family's sins, Barrick is the main course and three savory sides. Those eyes alone are enough to make me forget about a centuries' old feud and make nice."

"I have to go," I say as we rise higher into the air. "He's helping pilot the plane, but he'll be back here soon, and I need a second to figure out what I'm going to say."

"Don't confront him in the air," Bradford warns. "If he goes apeshit, you don't have anywhere to run. Wait until there are other people around, Trudy. Seriously. Better safe than sorry. Not even the rich and powerful can get away with killing people in public. But on a private plane that he can land anywhere he chooses to dispose of the body...not so much."

"Okay. Goodbye. I love you," I say, my throat so tight I can barely force out the words. "Tell Millie and the baby I love them if something happens, okay? And make sure the foundation stays in the black." I end the call before Bradford can reply.

The door to the cockpit could open at any second.

When it does, I'll have to decide—trust my friend who's always given me good advice or trust the dreamy voice inside that insists Sterling isn't faking the connection that's building between us. He's a finance guy not a trained actor and I'm not that easy to fool, not when it comes to feelings.

Are you willing to bet your life on that?

I bite my lip, anxiety clutching at my throat, as the handle on the cockpit entrance dips and the door begins to open.

Looks like I'm about to find out.

Trudy and Sterling's dark romance
concludes in
SAVING STERLING.

Subscribe to Everly's newsletter HERE
and never miss a sale or new release!

ABOUT THE AUTHOR

EVERLY STONE writes dark, dangerous, action-packed romance. Love Dominant Alpha males and strong women who know what they want—in bed and out of it?

Dive into the Bought by the Billionaire series! Learn more at Everly's site https://www.everlystone.com.

Everly also writes sexy contemporary romance and laugh out loud romantic comedy as Lili Valente.

Learn more at www.lilivalente.com

ALSO BY EVERLY STONE

Learn more at Everly's website

https://www.everlystone.com.

* * *

Sold to Sterling

(Must be read in order)

Sold to Sterling

Serving Sterling

Saving Sterling

Bought by the Billionaire

The Series

(HOT novellas, must be read in order)

Dark Domination

Deep Domination

Desperate Domination

Divine Domination

Kidnapped by the Billionaire

The Series

(HOT novellas, must be read in order)

Filthy Wicked Love

Crazy Beautiful Love

One More Shameless Night

Under His Command

The Series

(HOT novellas, must be read in order)

Controlling her Pleasure

Commanding her Trust

Claiming her Heart

The Snowed in Series

Snowbound with the Billionaire

Snowed in with the Boss

www.ingramcontent.com/pod-product-compliance
Lightning Source LLC
Chambersburg PA
CBHW071617150726

48000CB00004B/1761